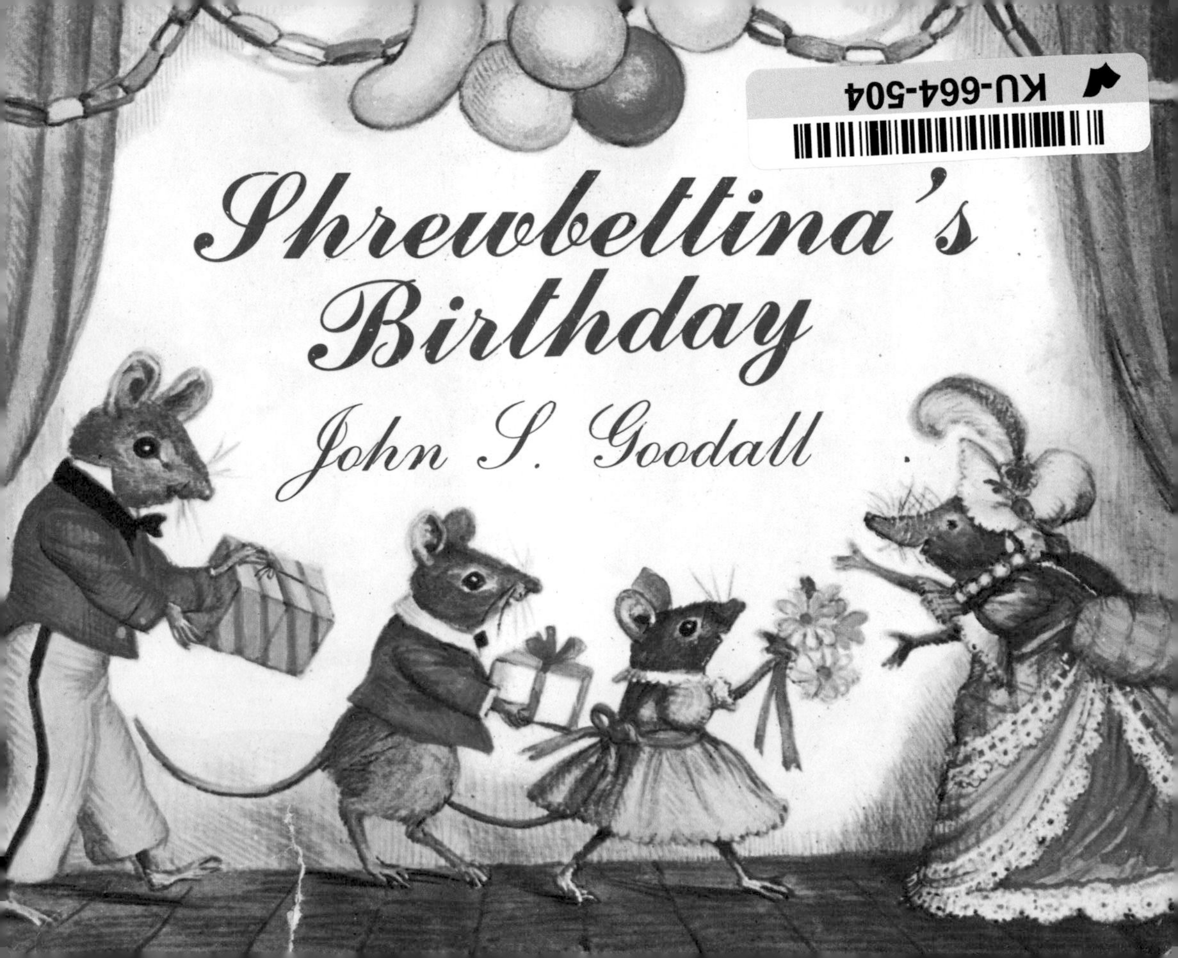
Shrewbettina's Birthday
John S. Goodall

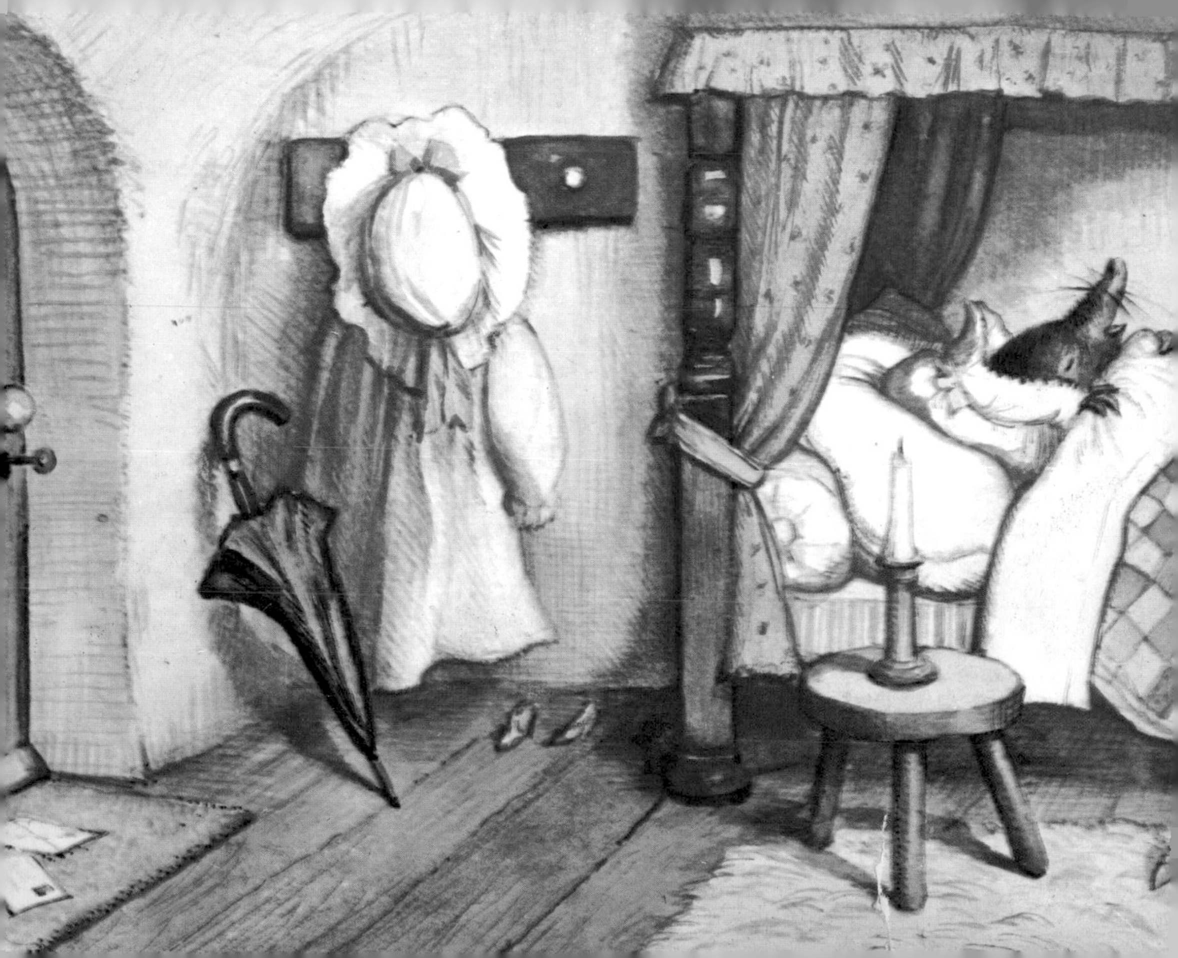

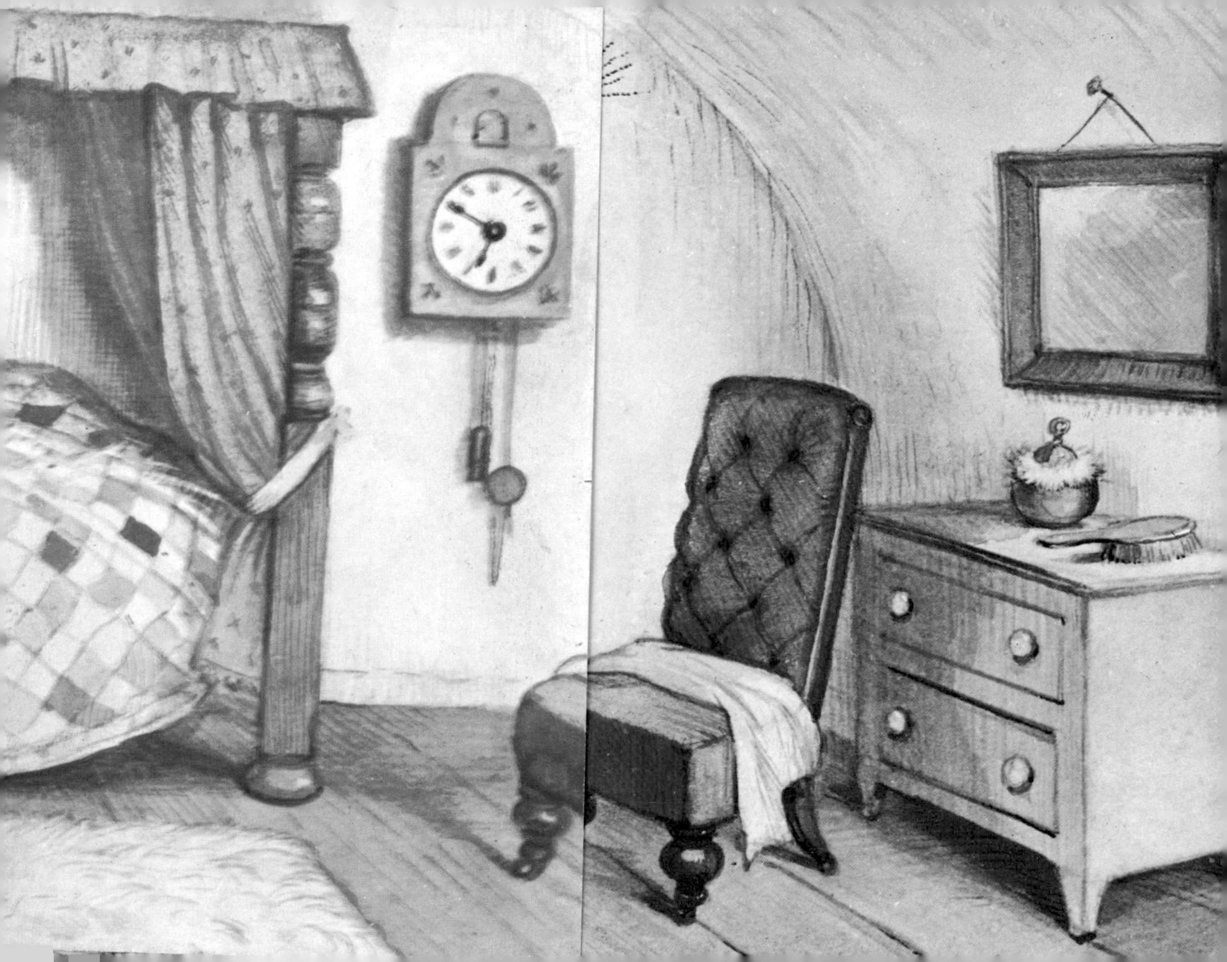

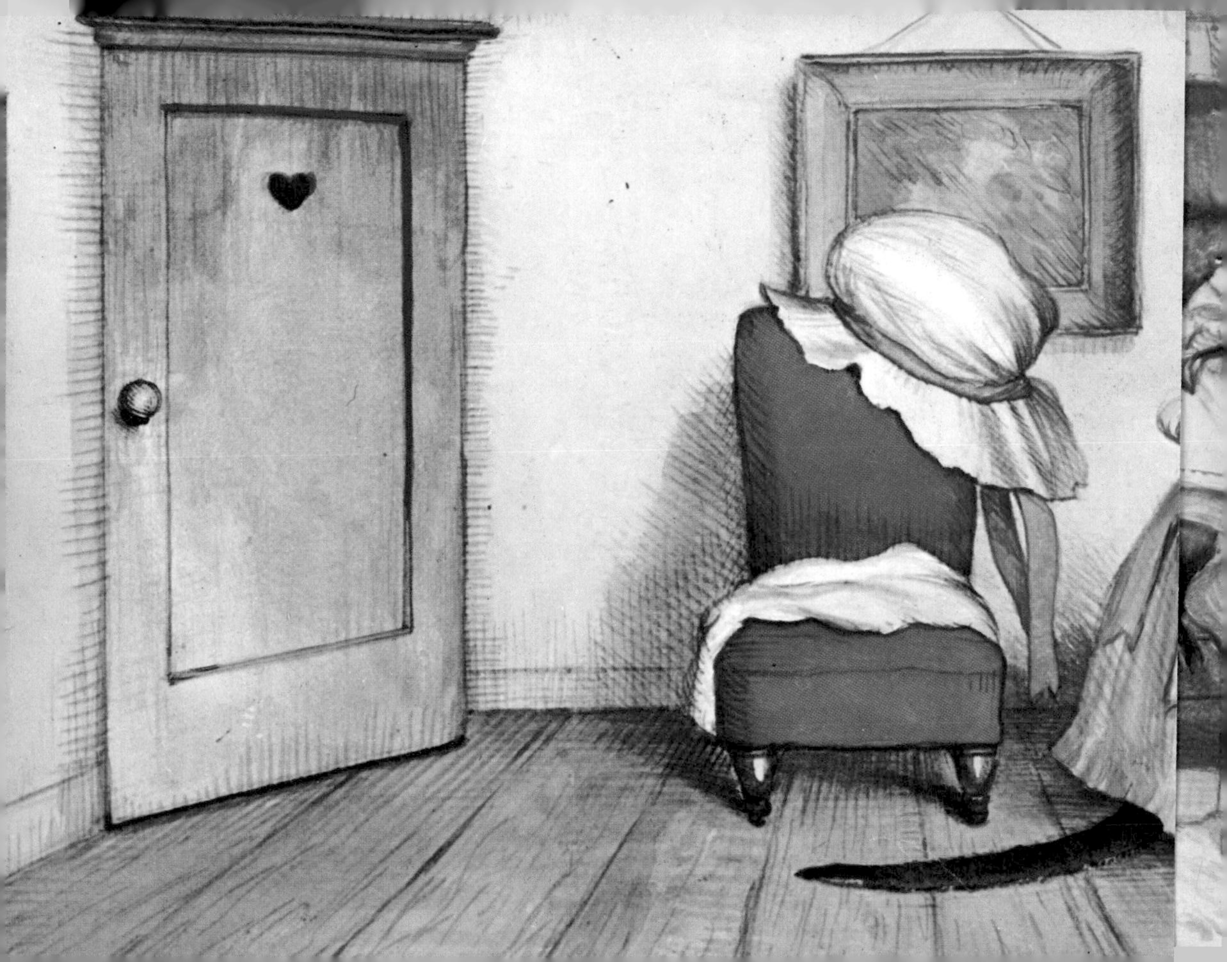

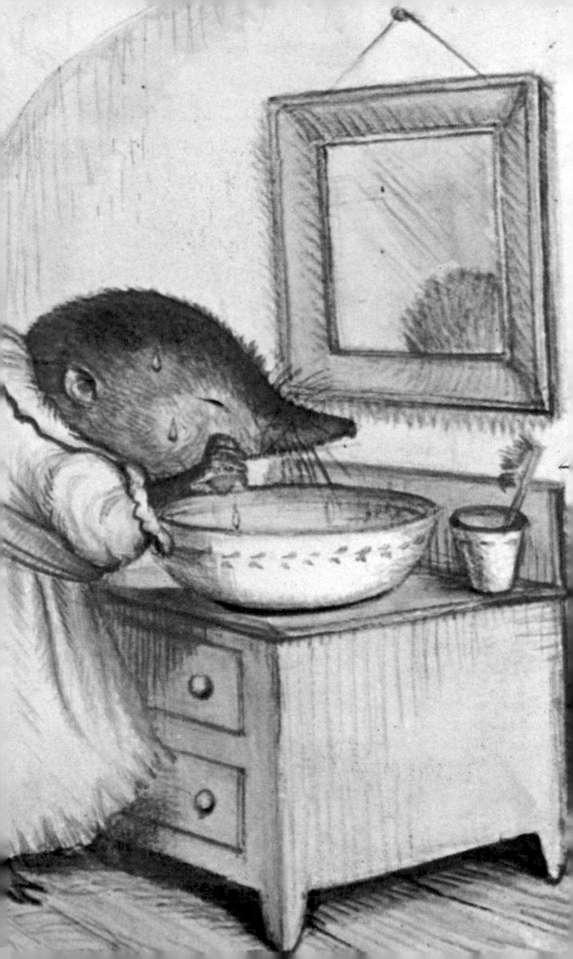

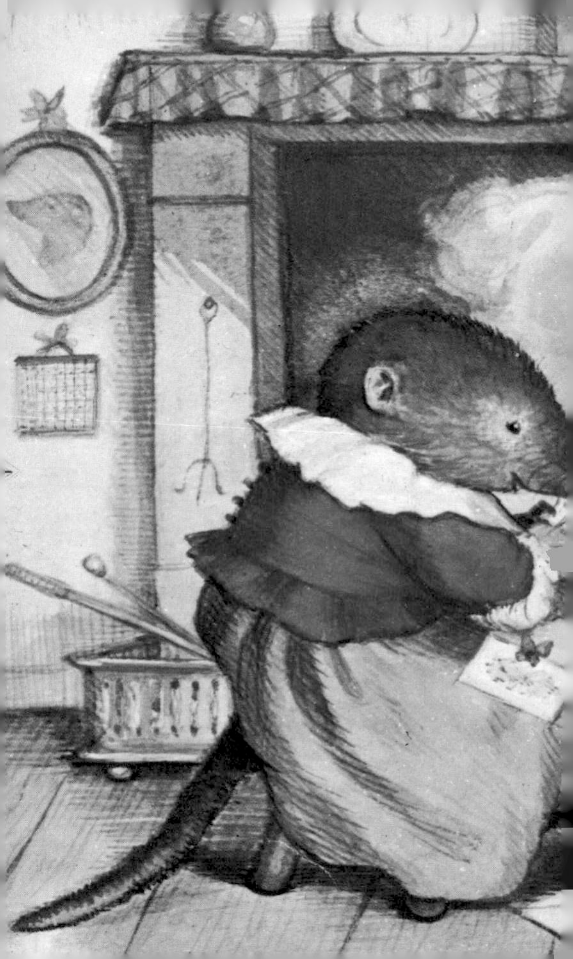

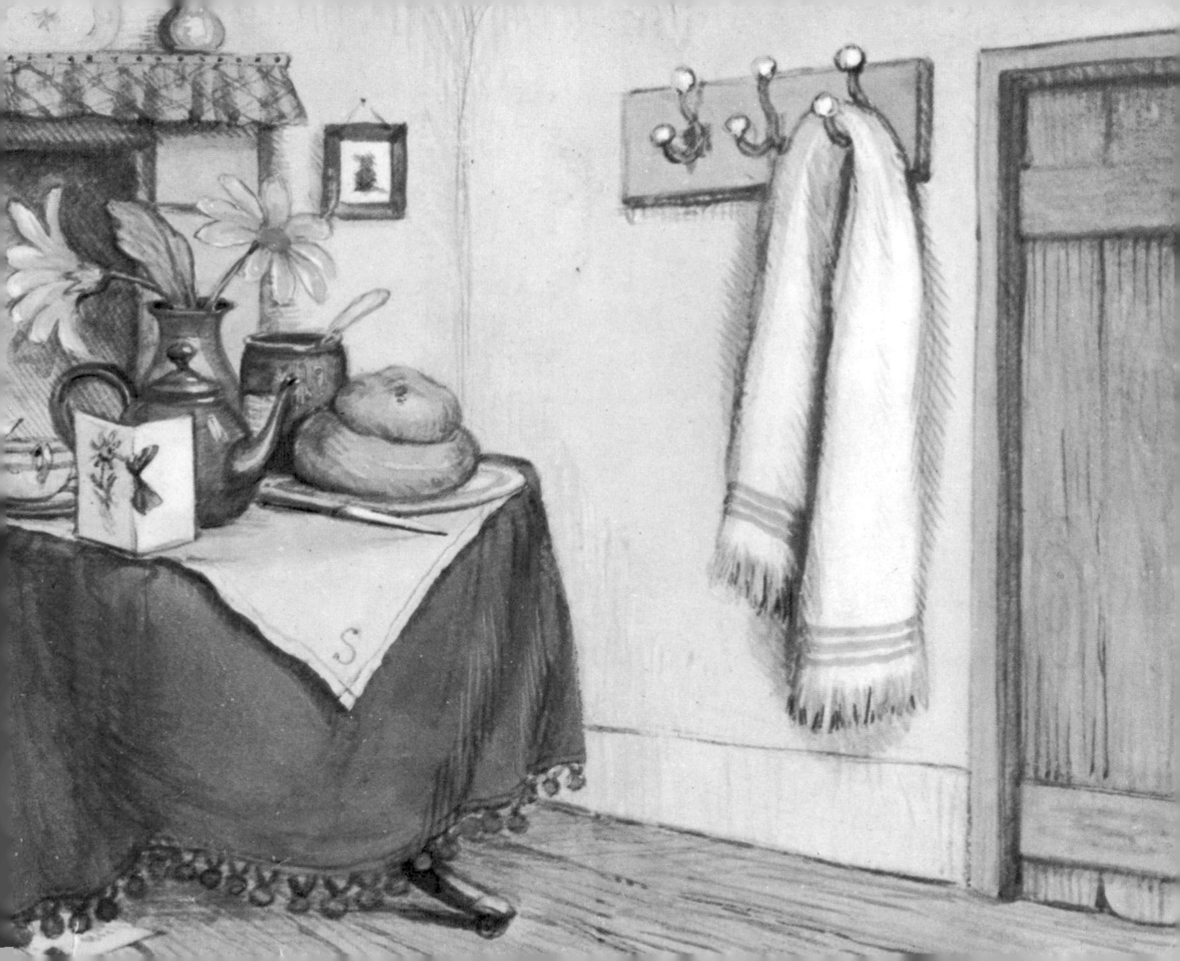

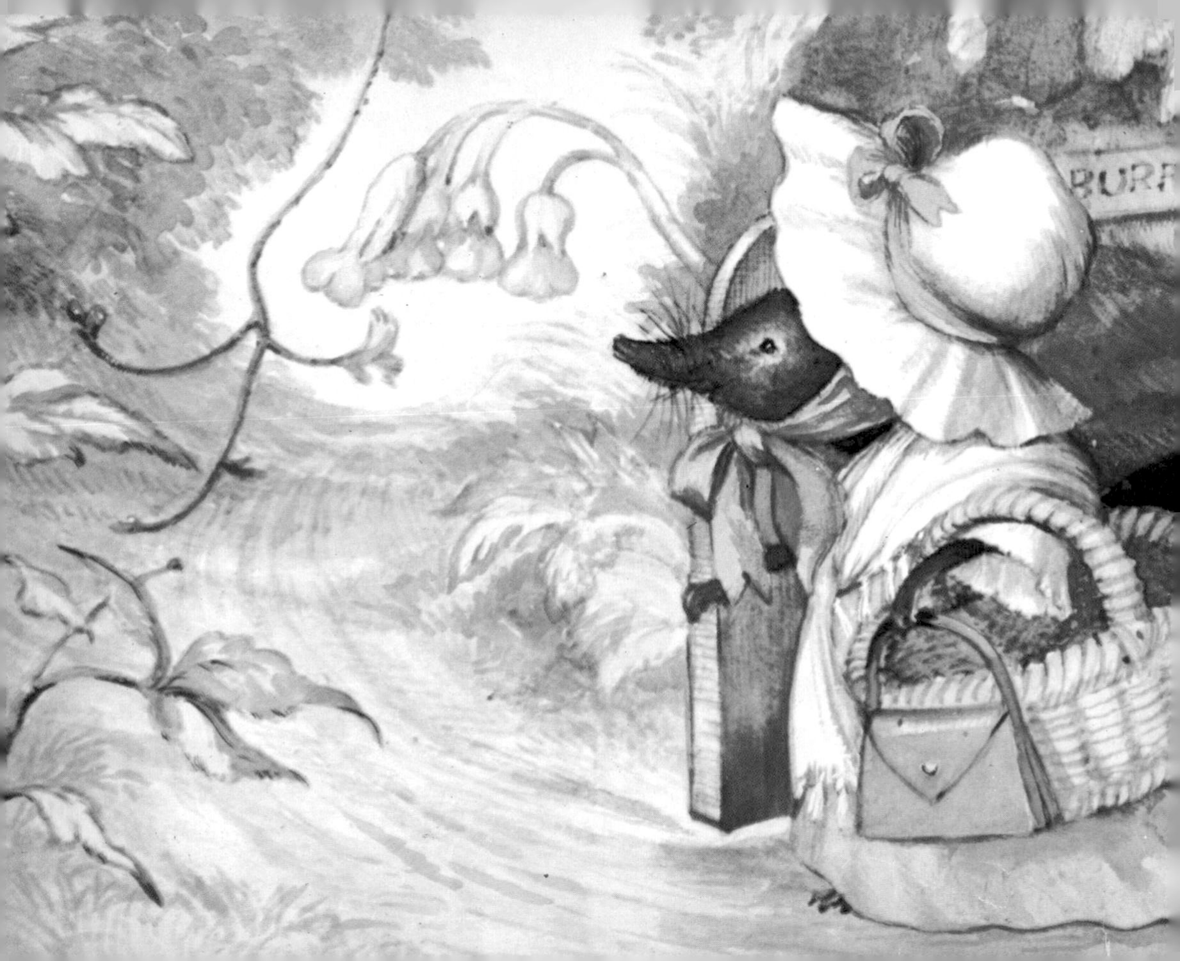

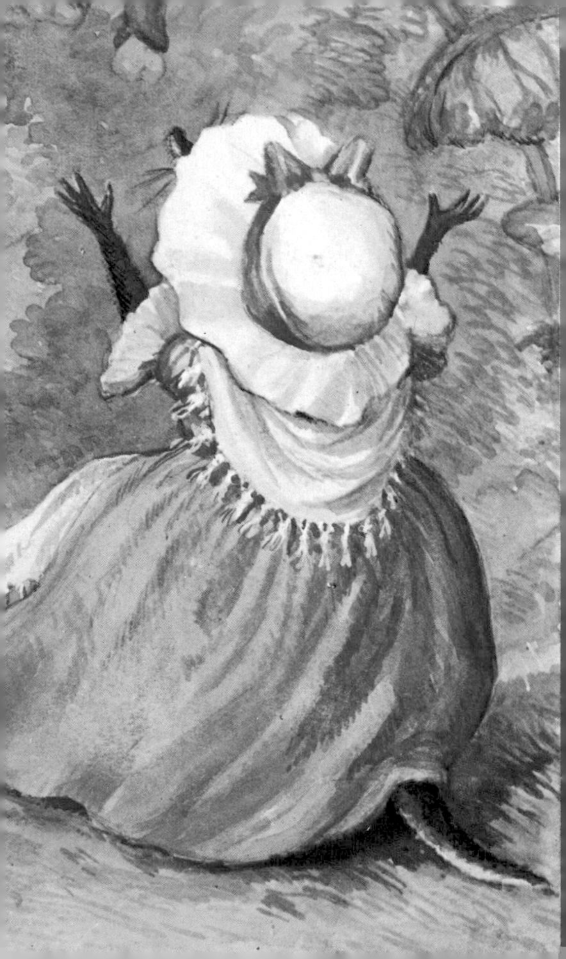

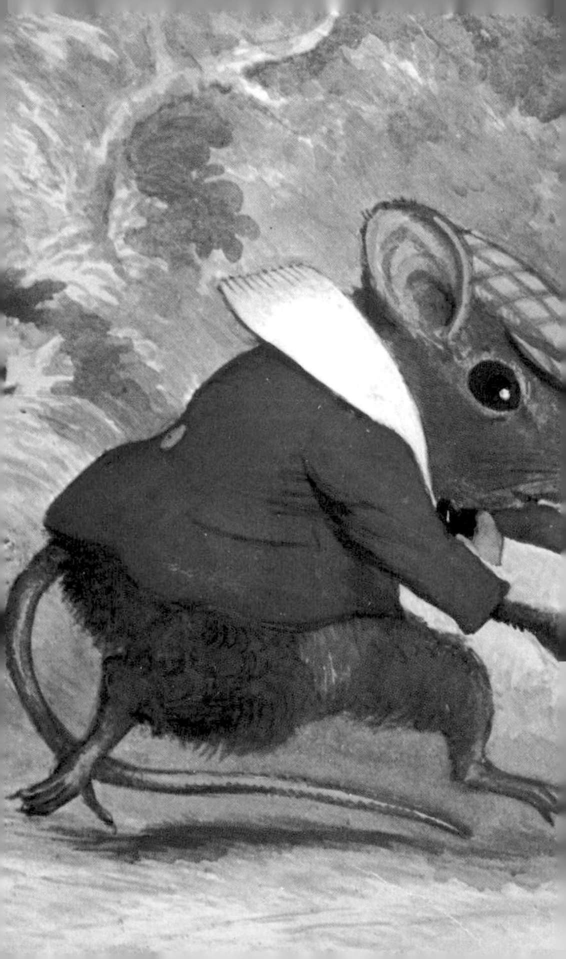

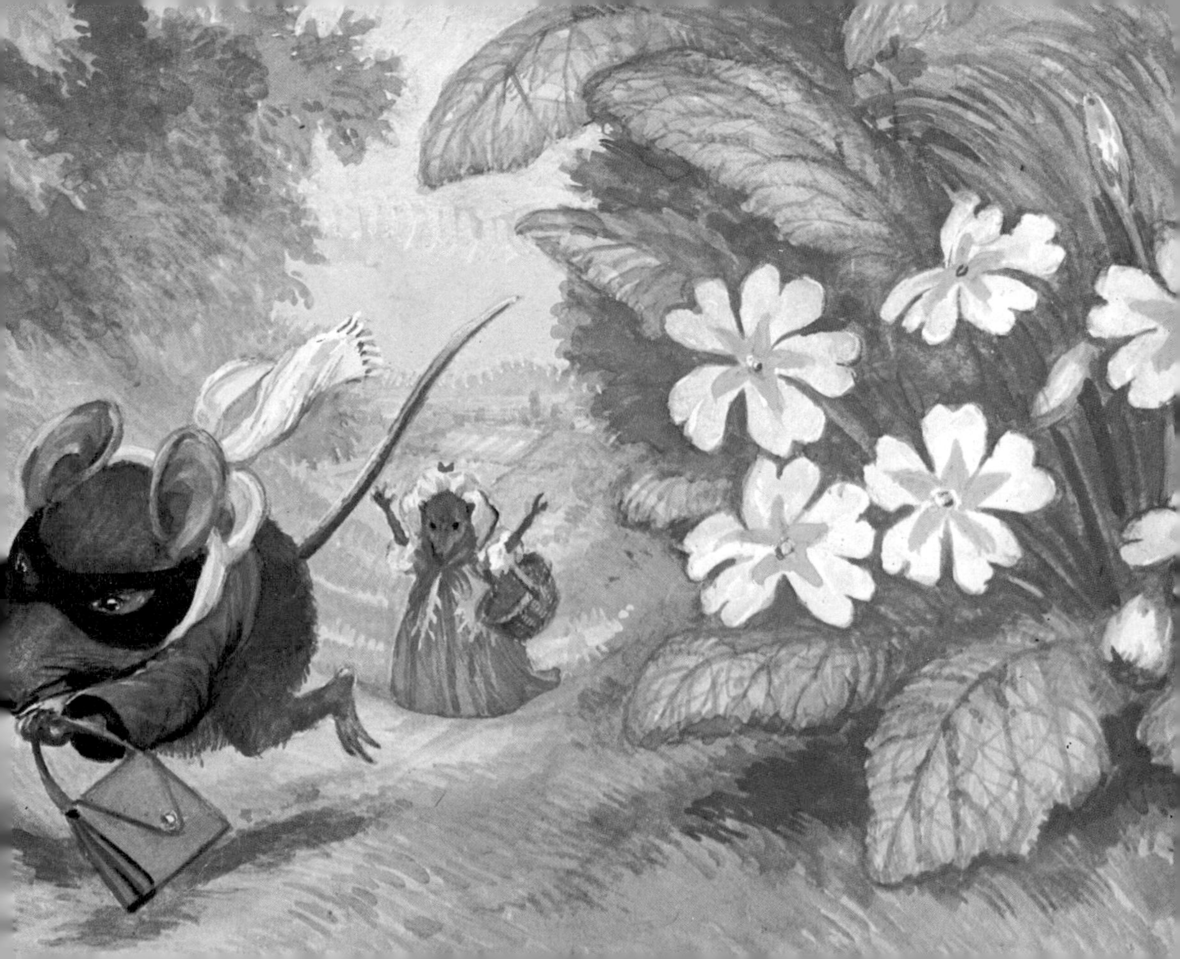

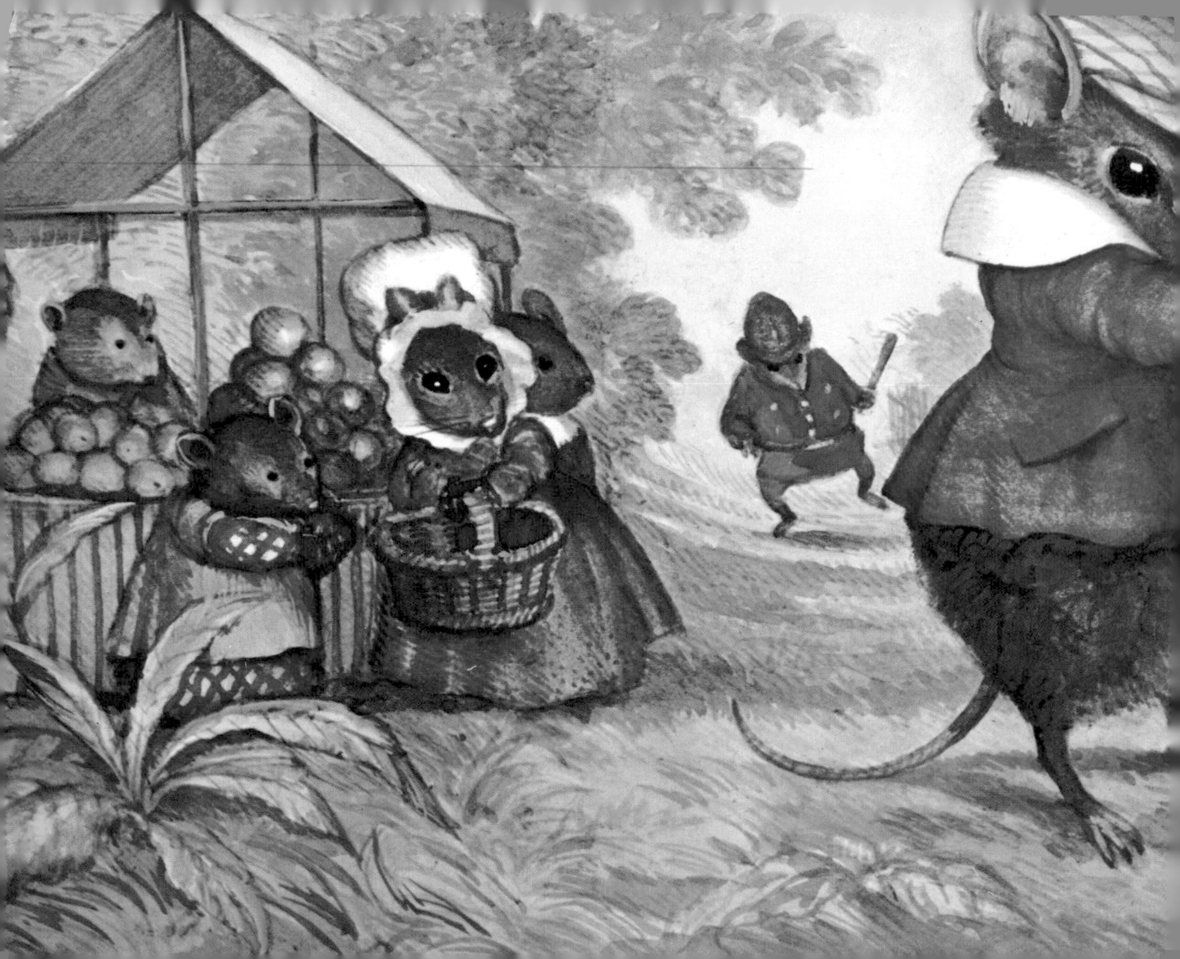

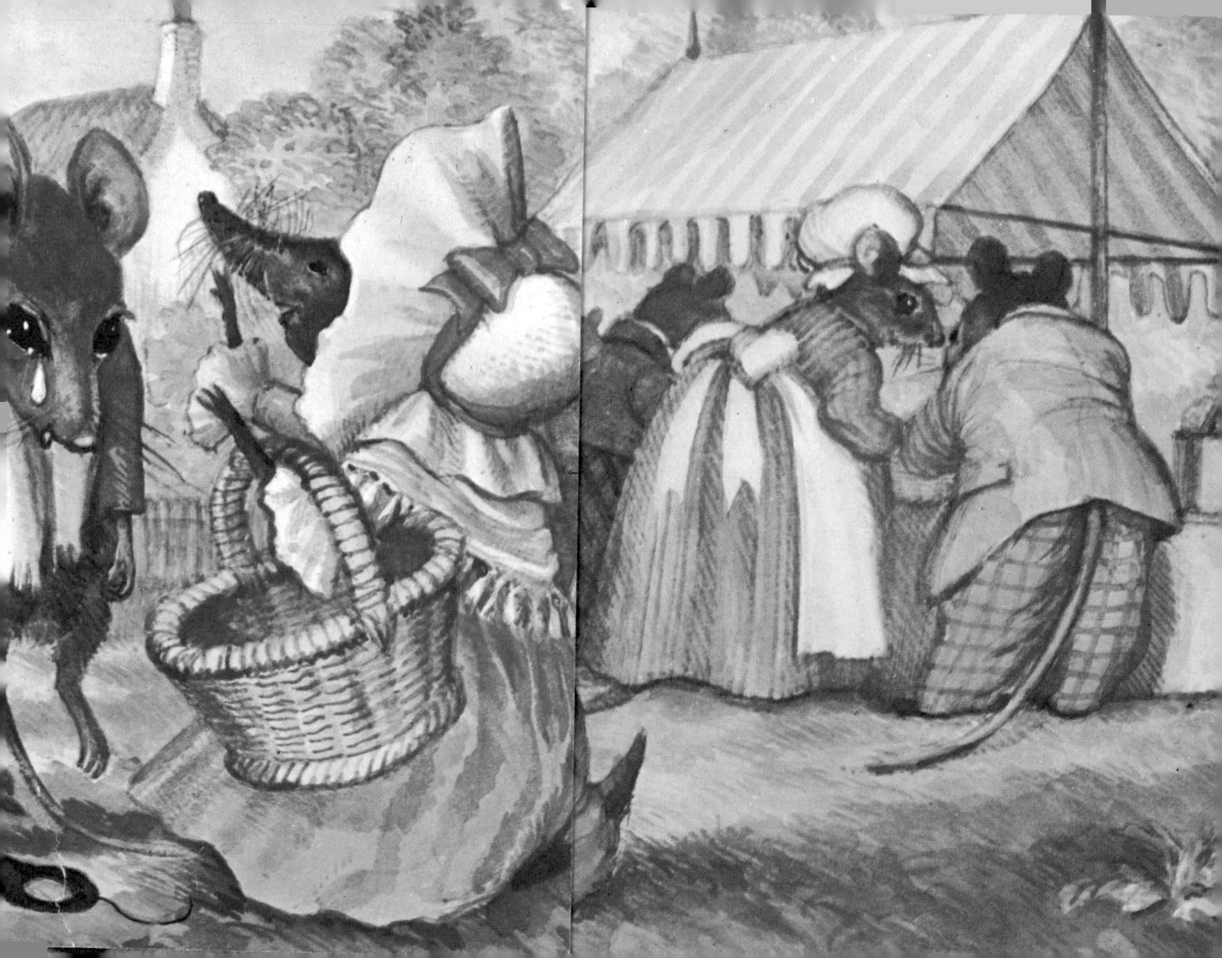

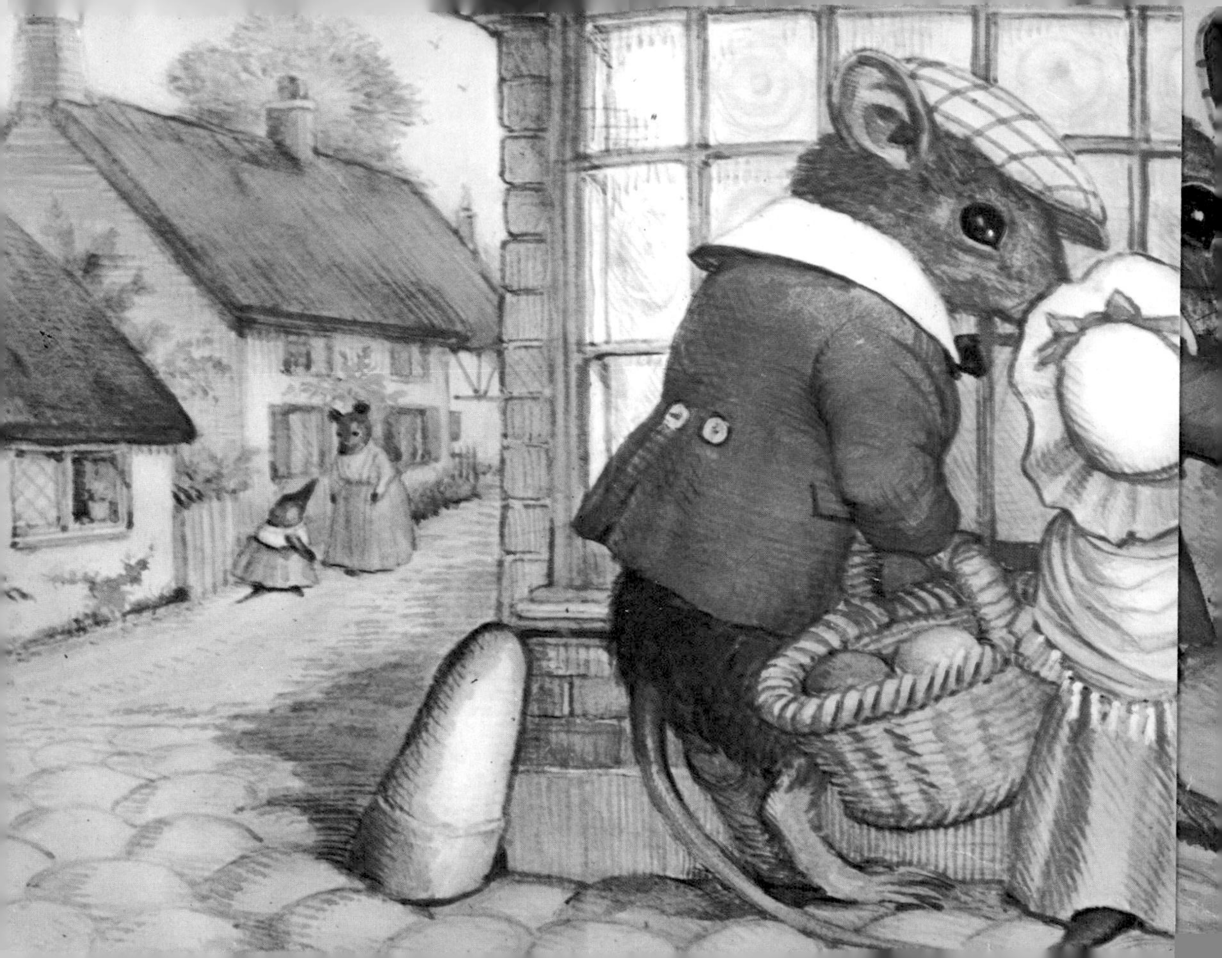

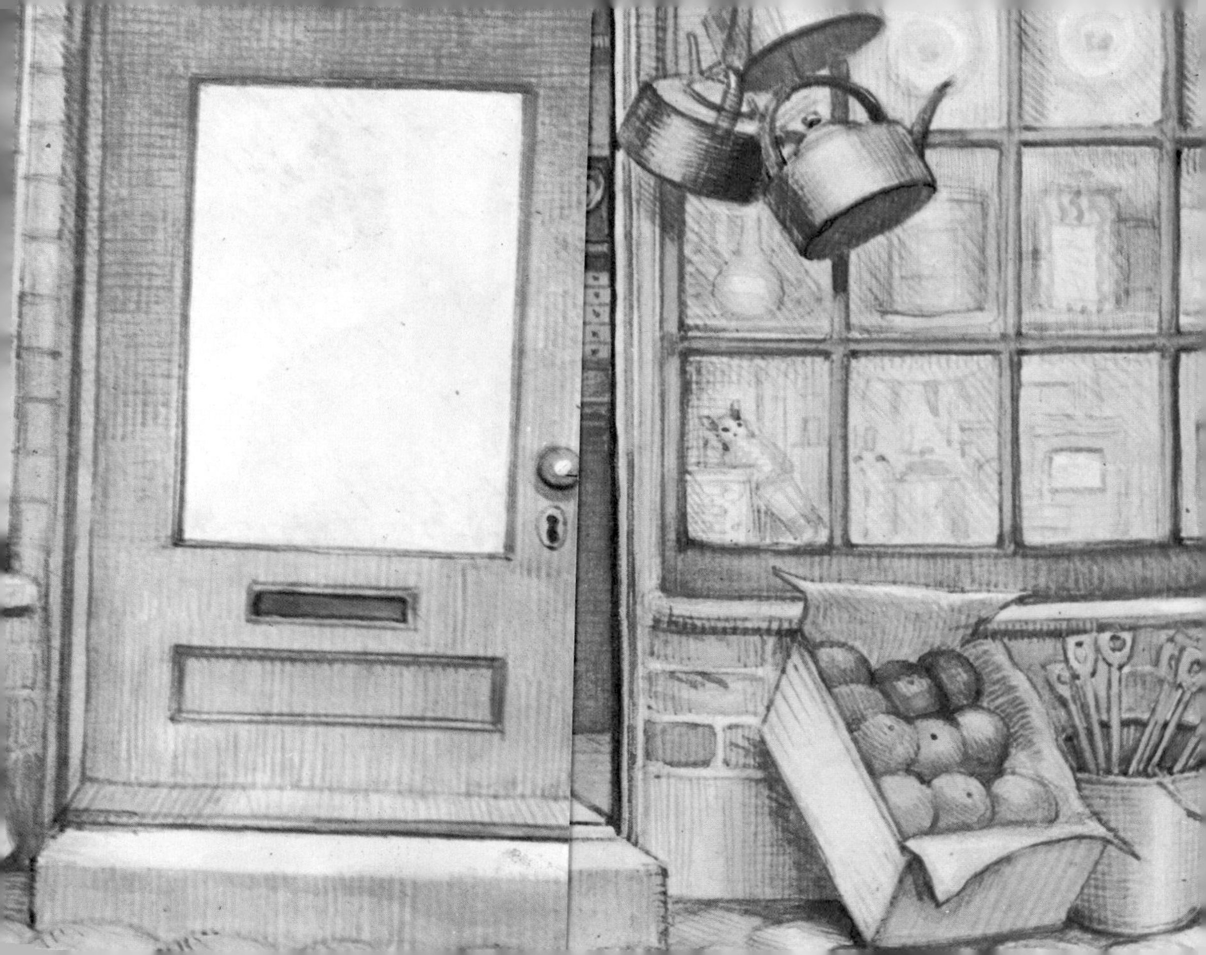

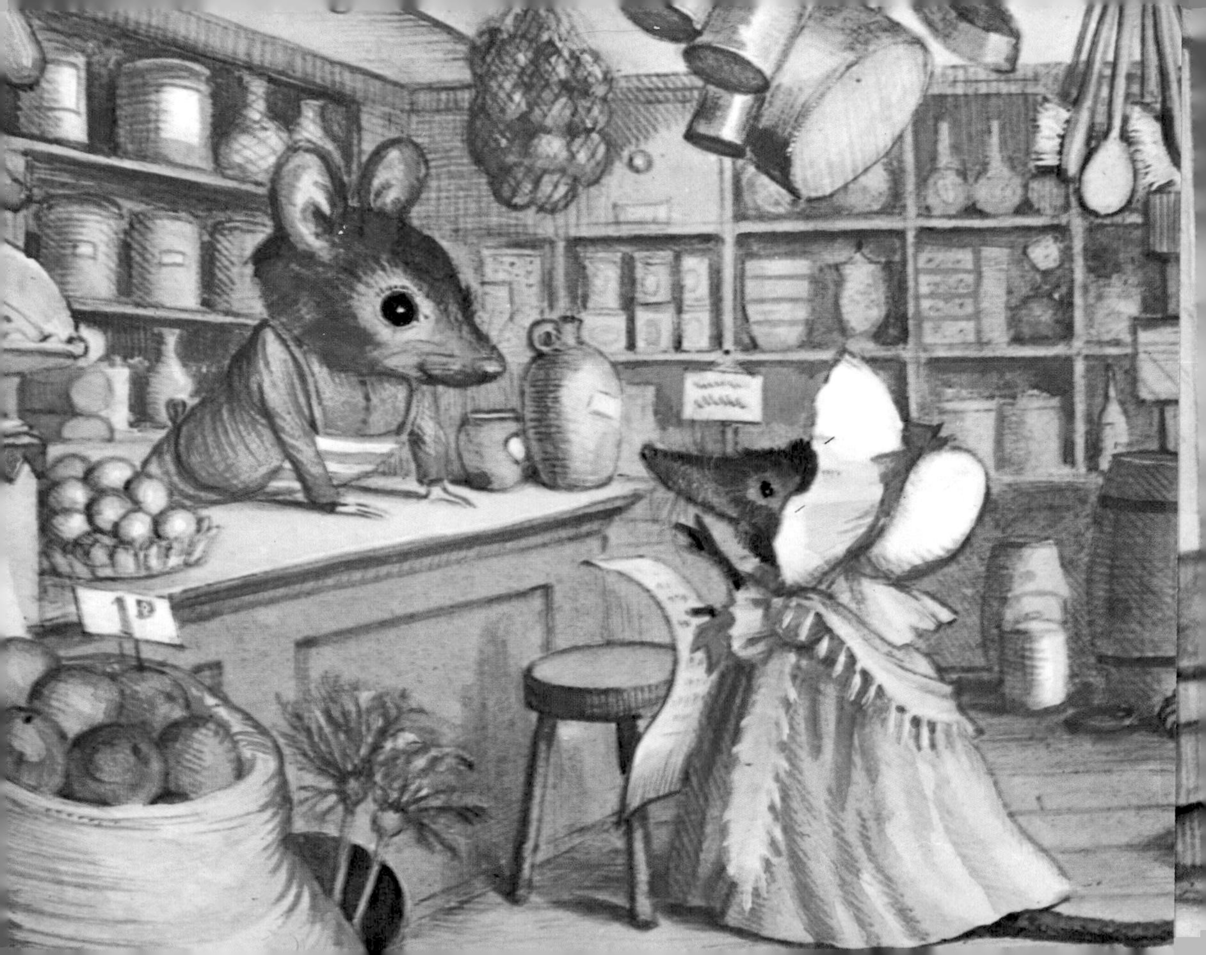
1P

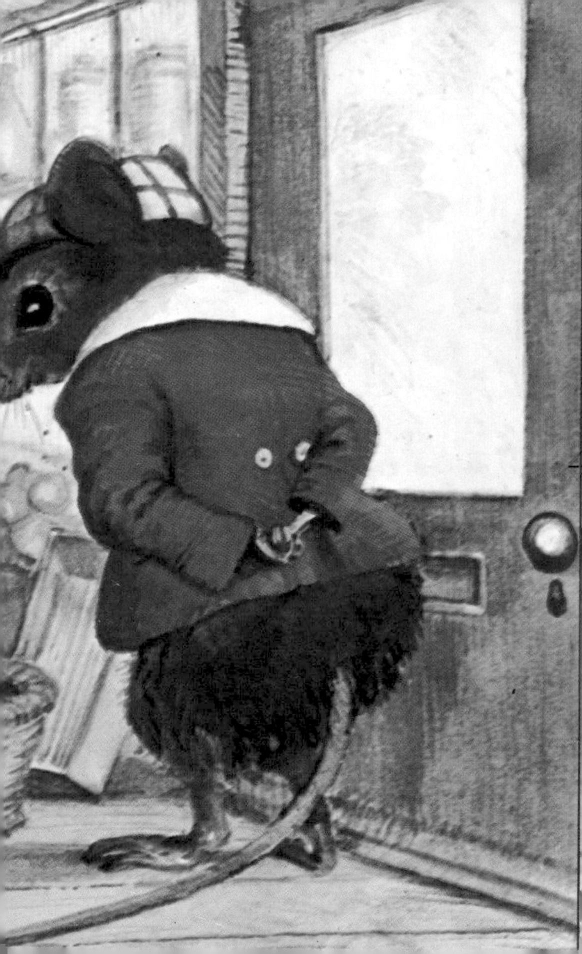

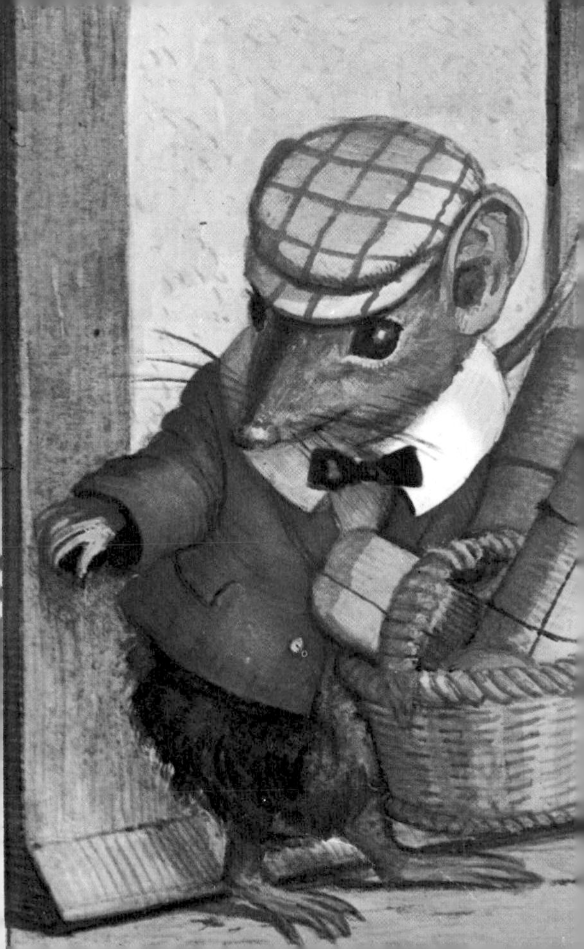

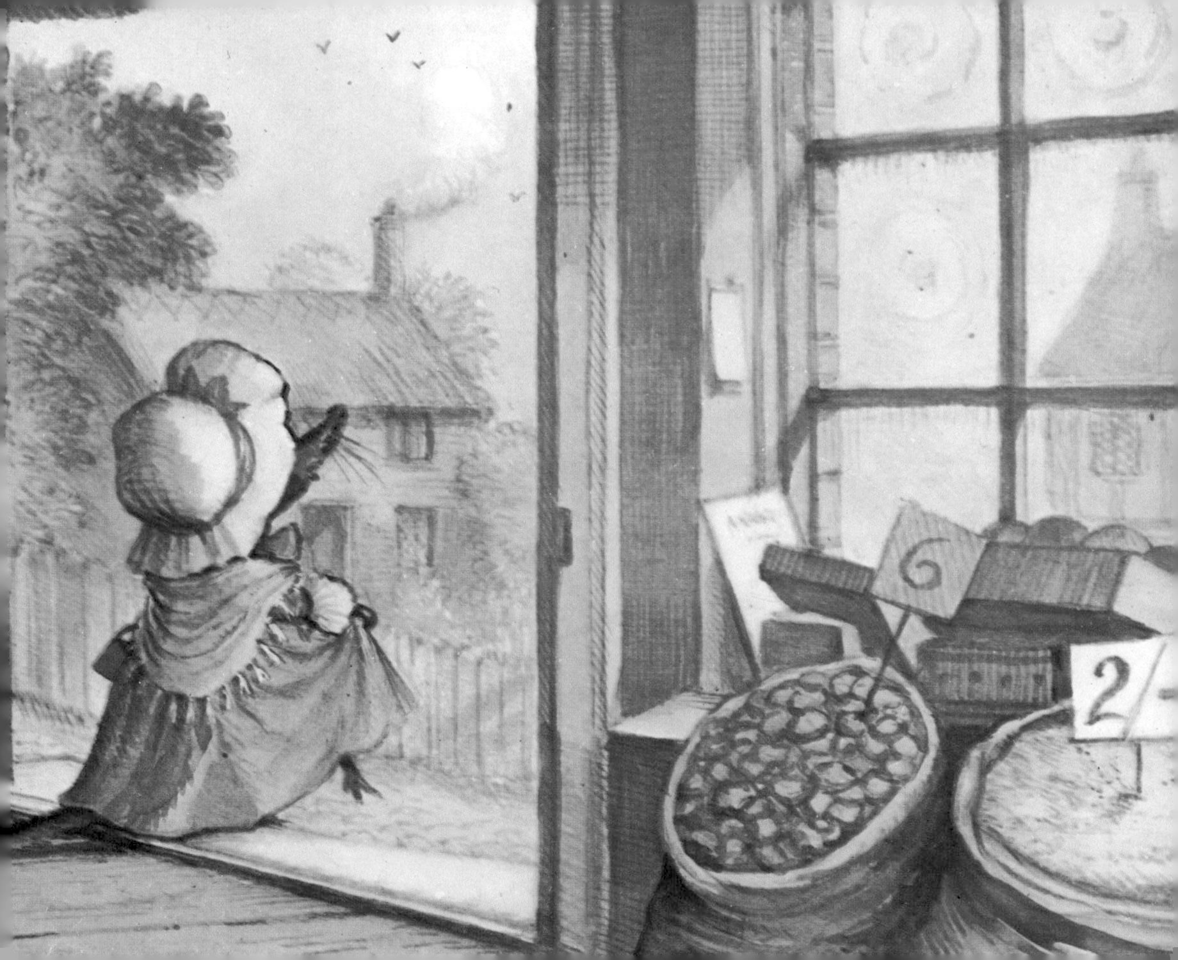
6
2/

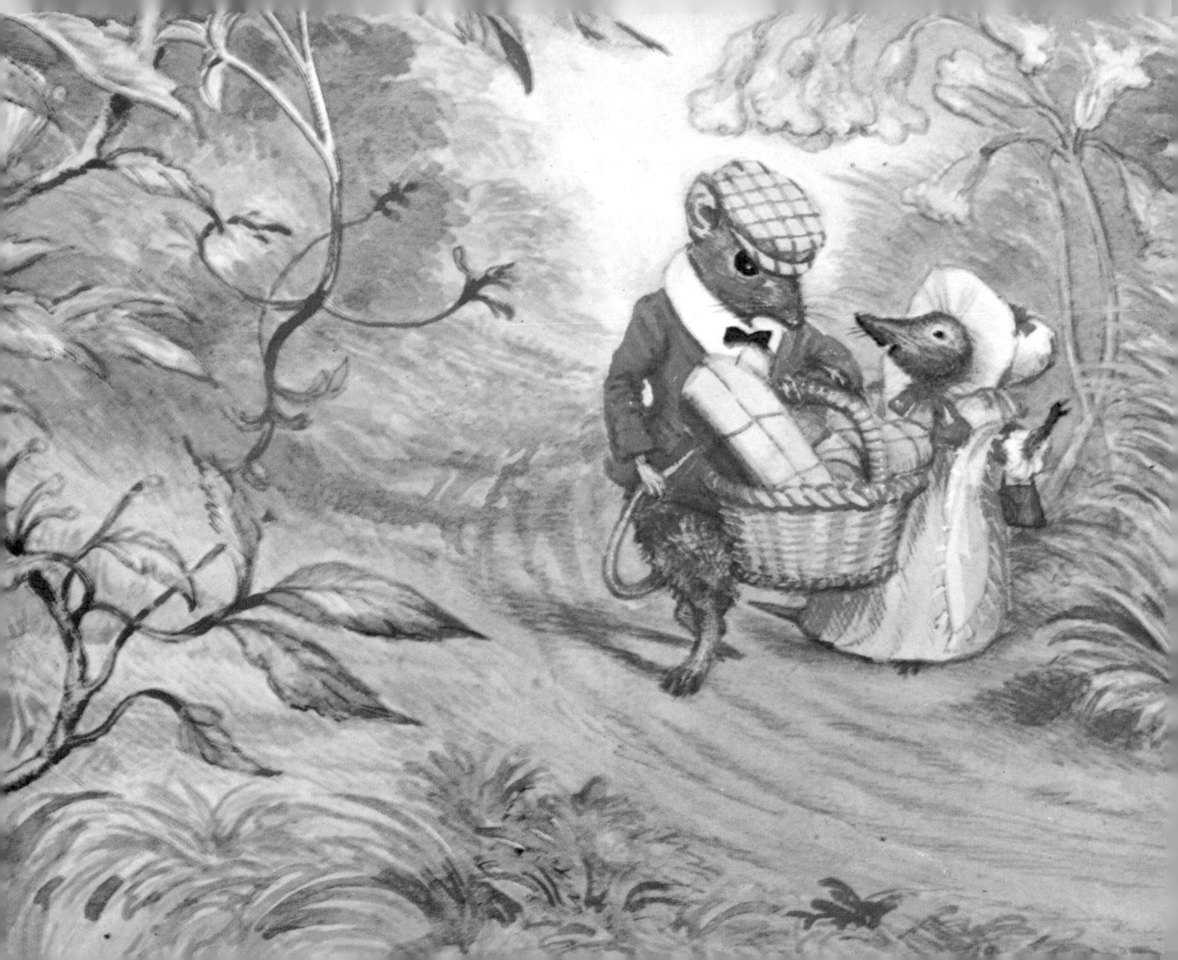

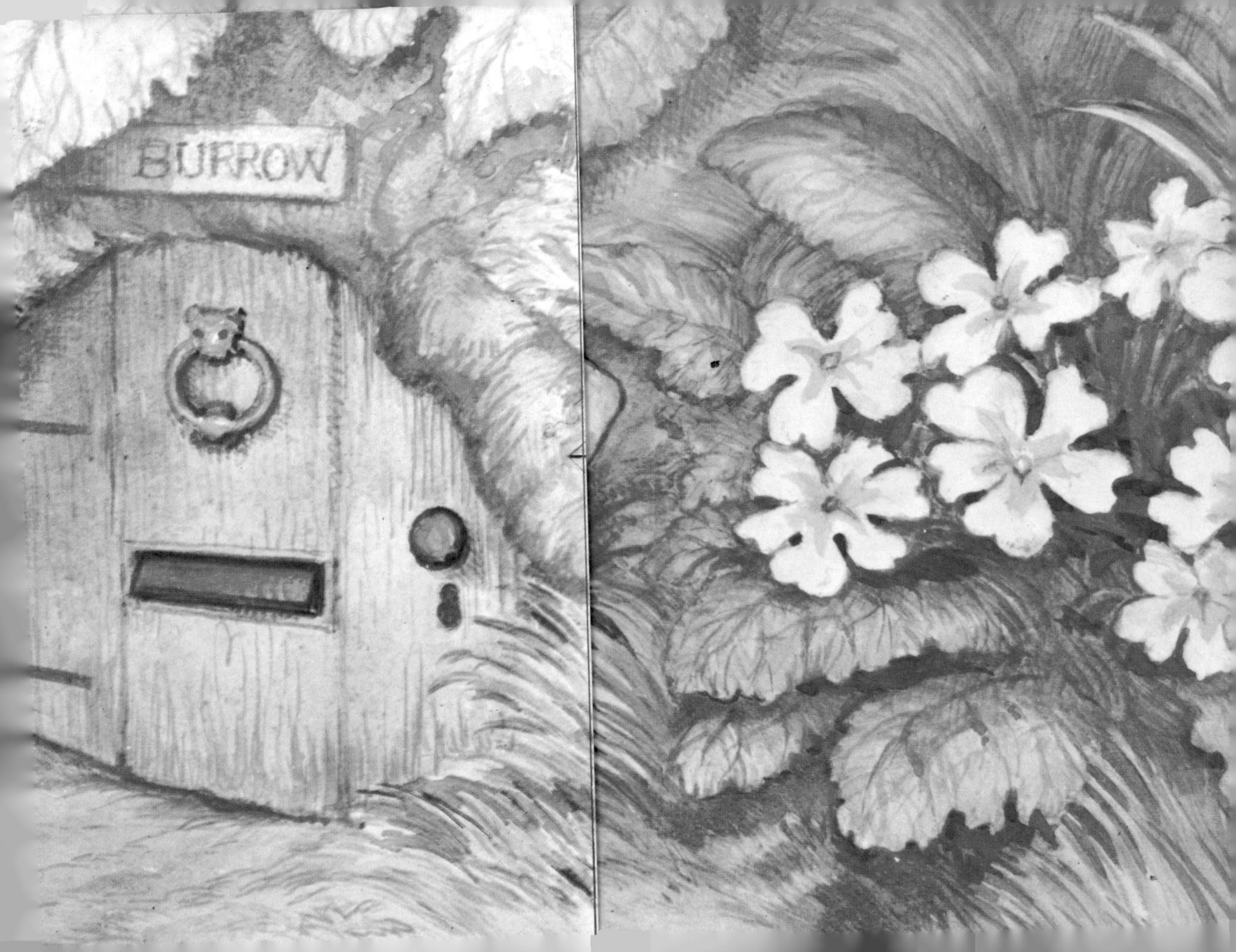
BURROW

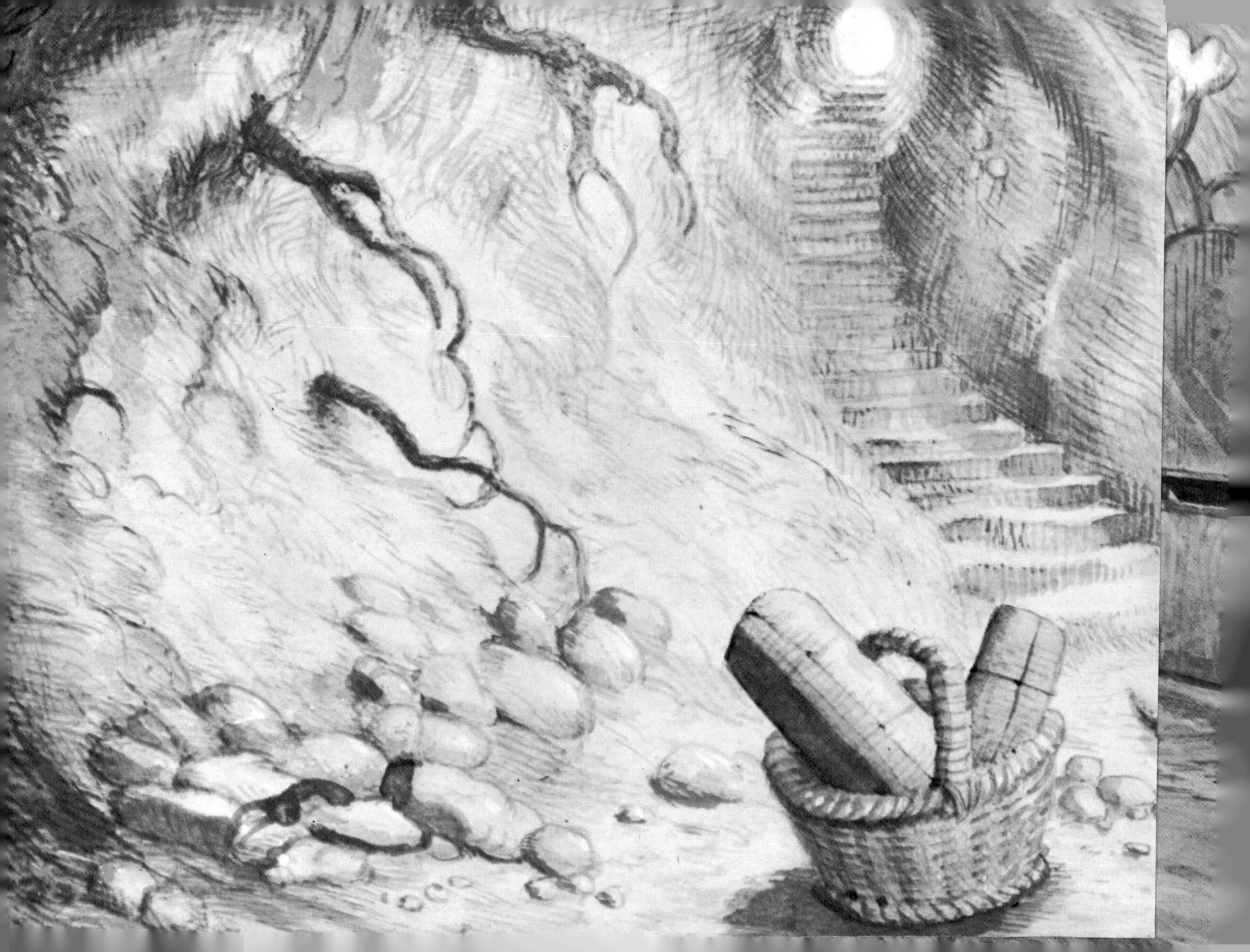

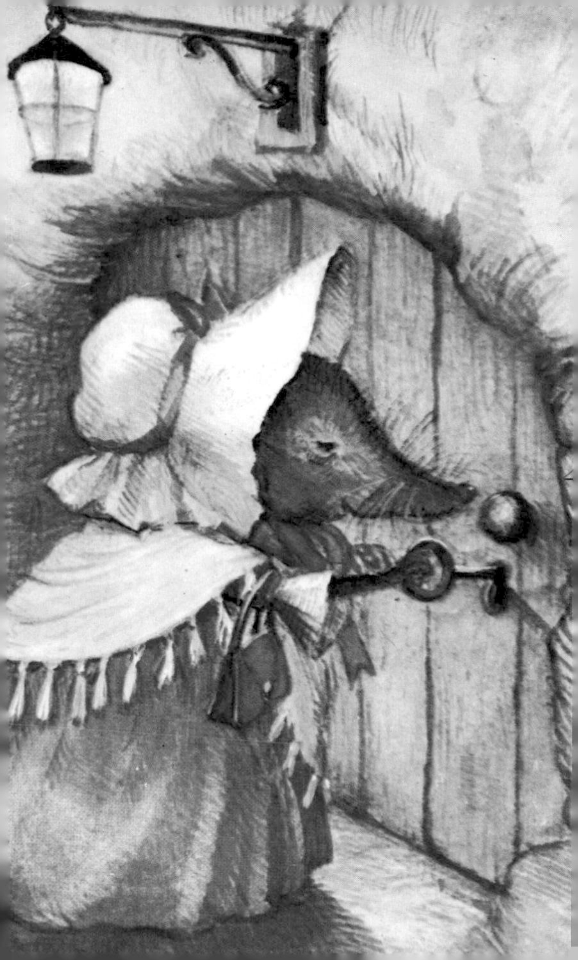

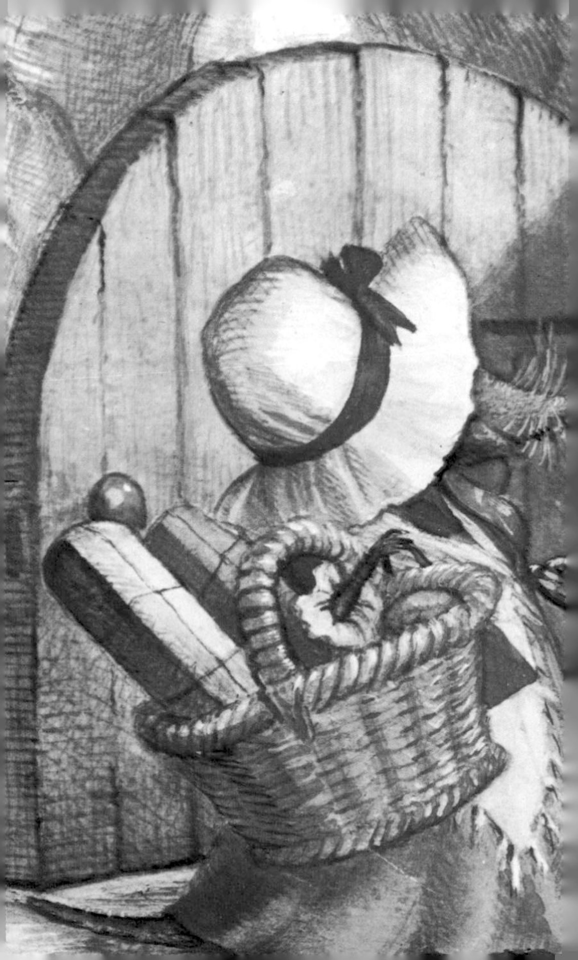

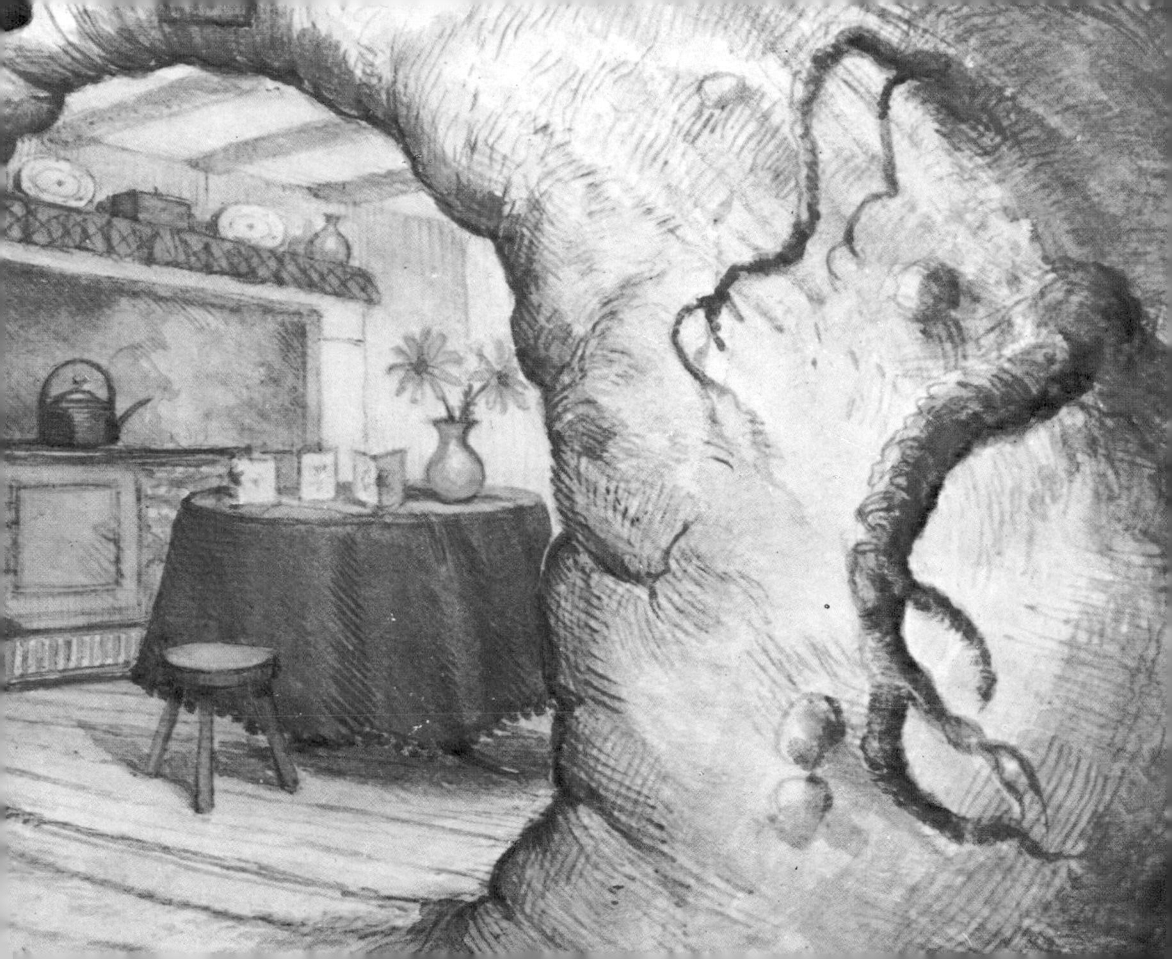

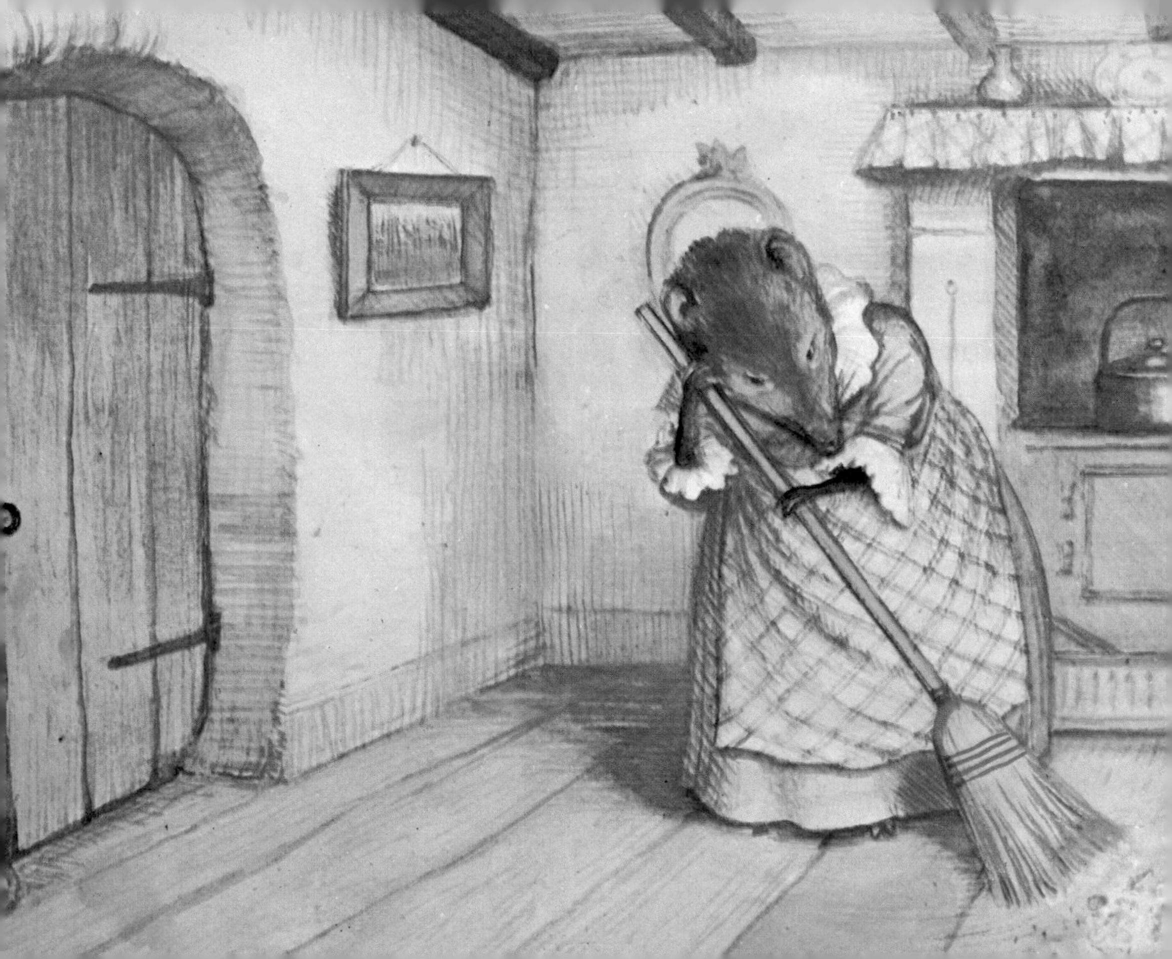

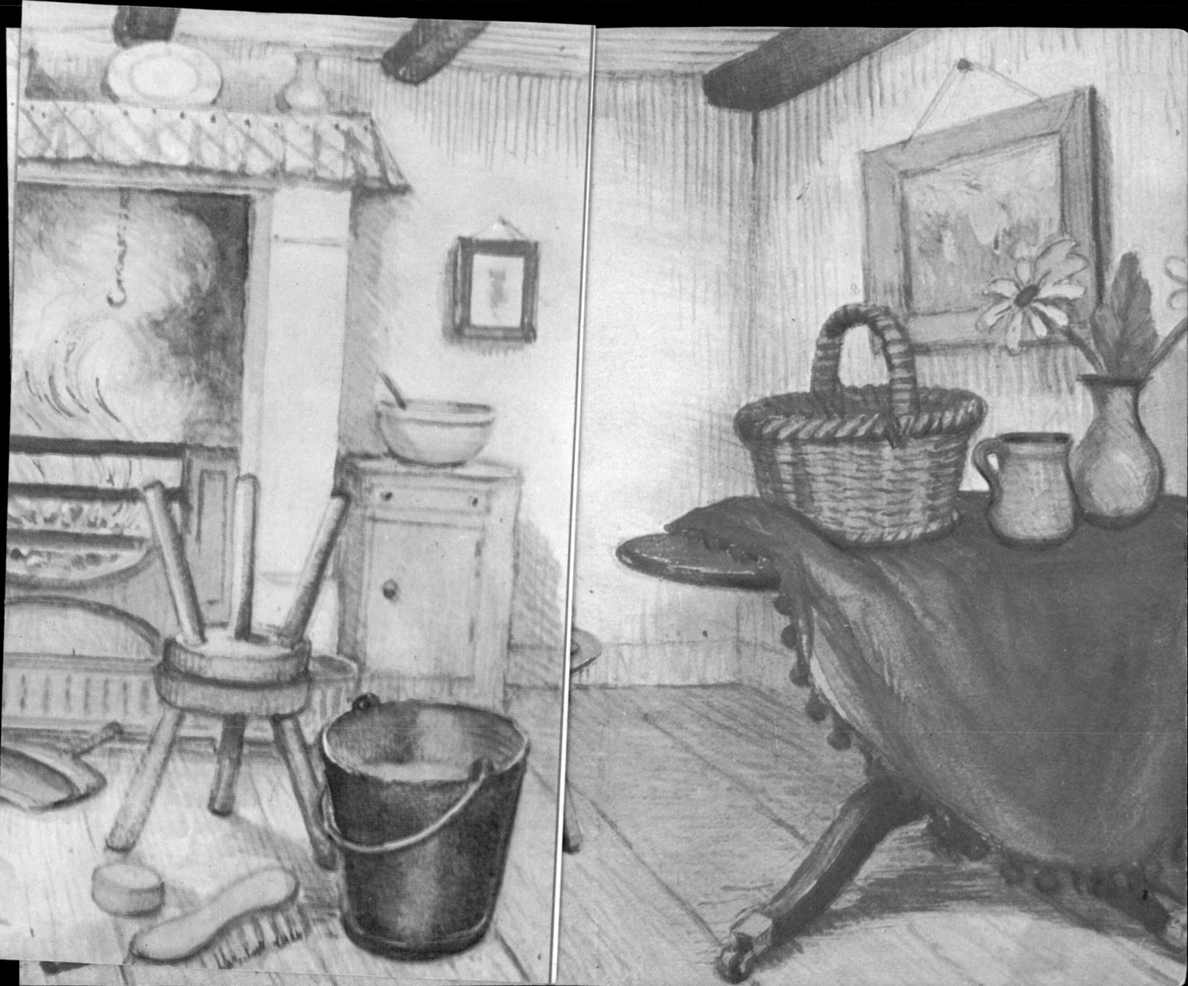

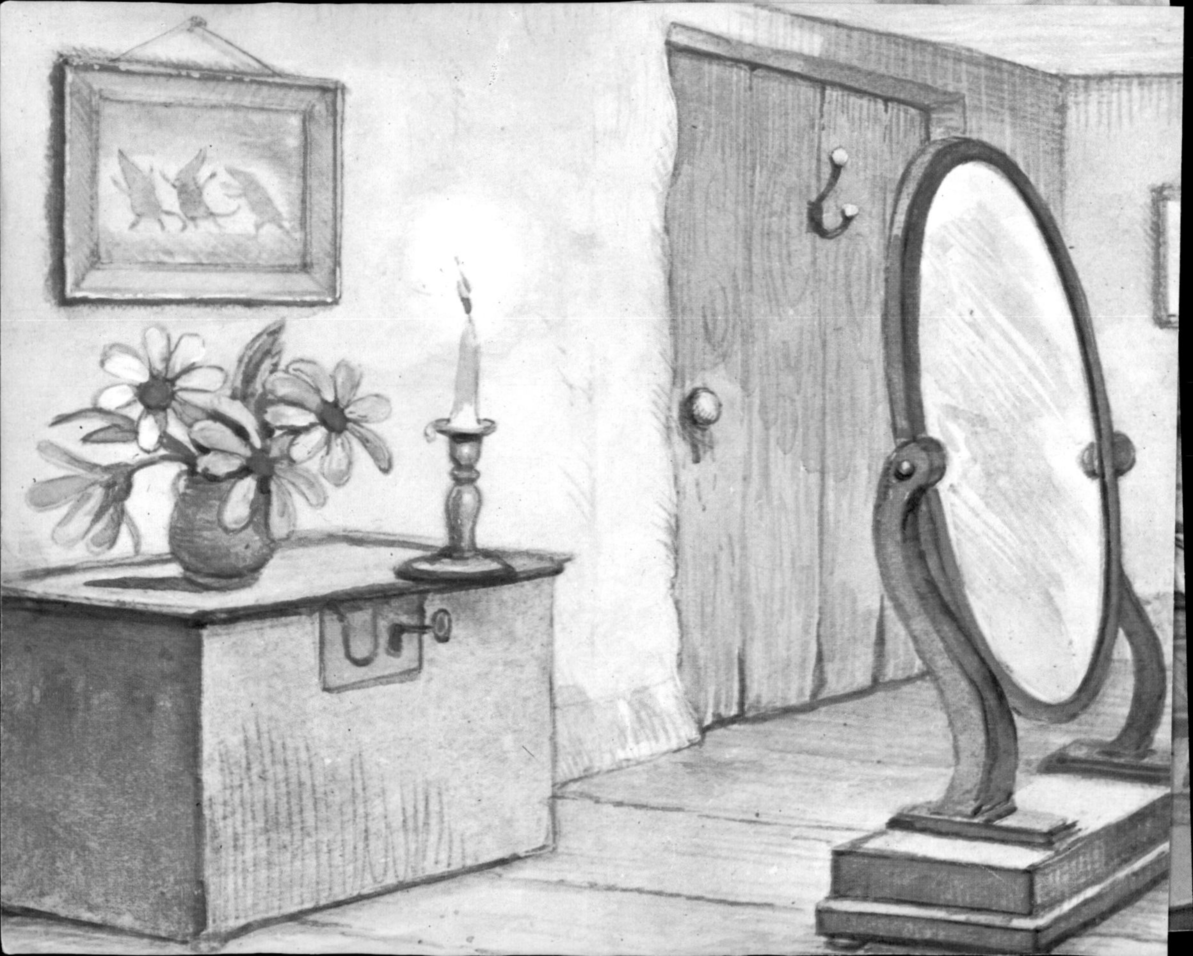

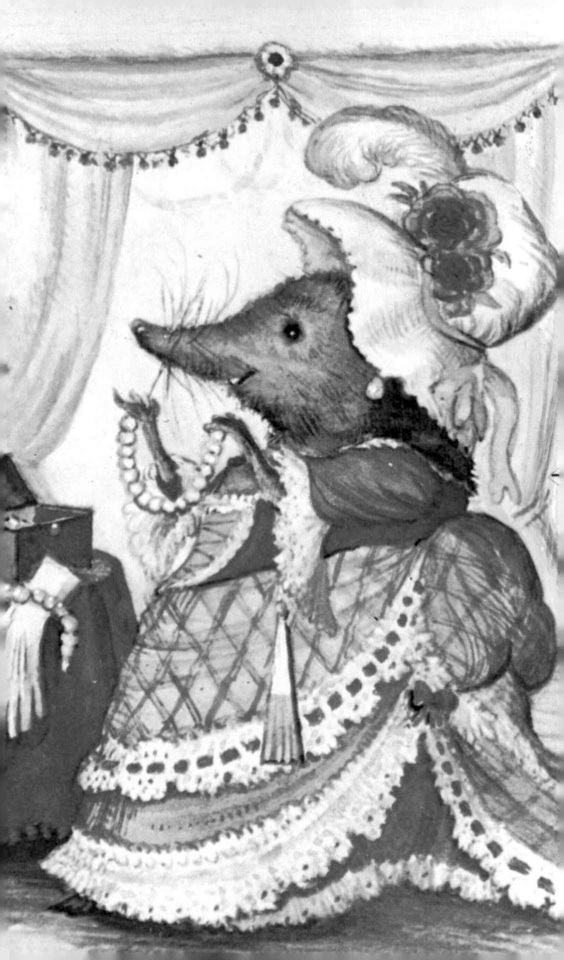

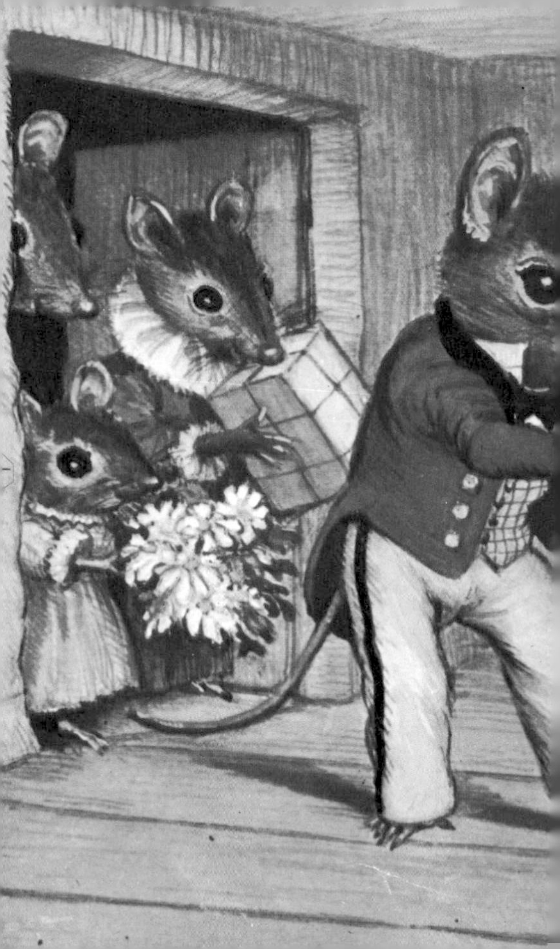

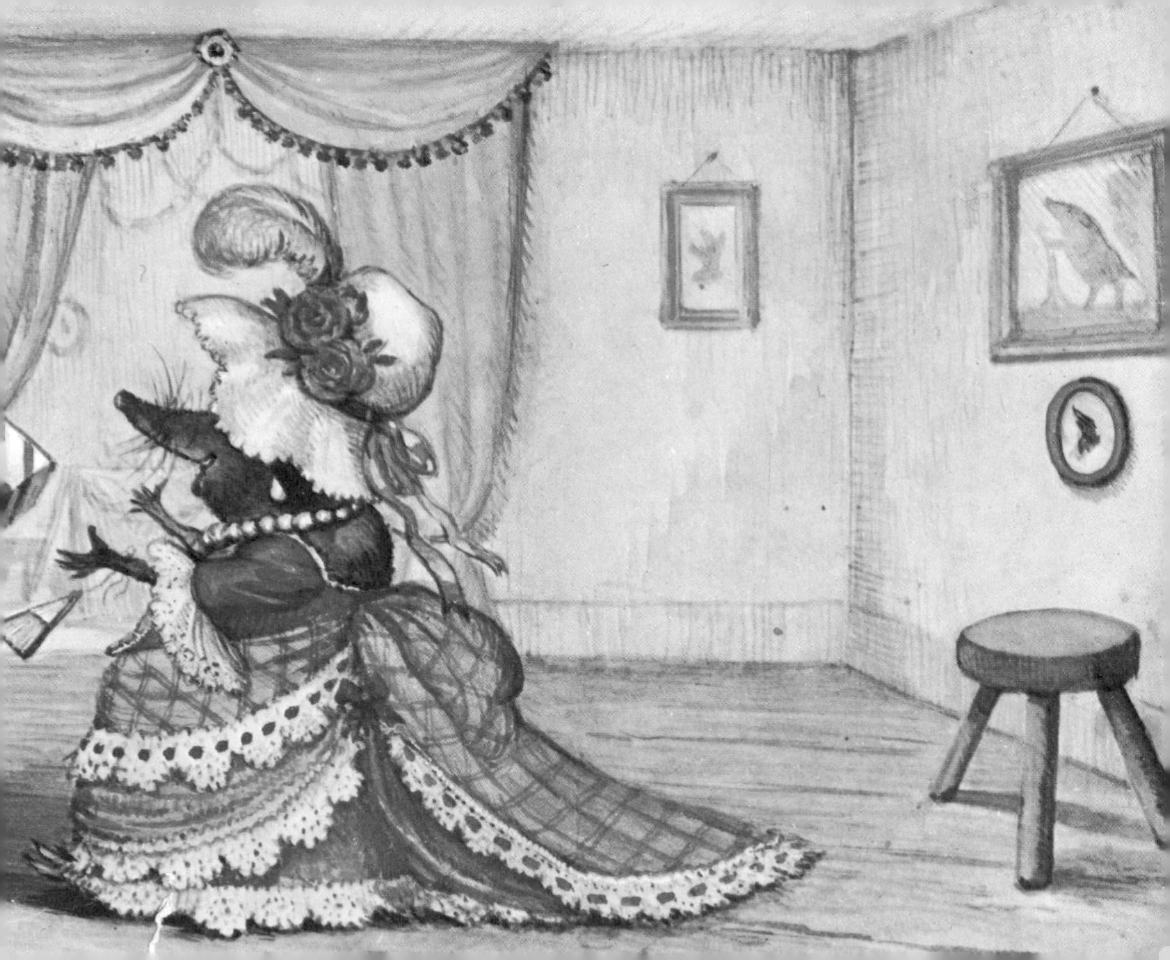

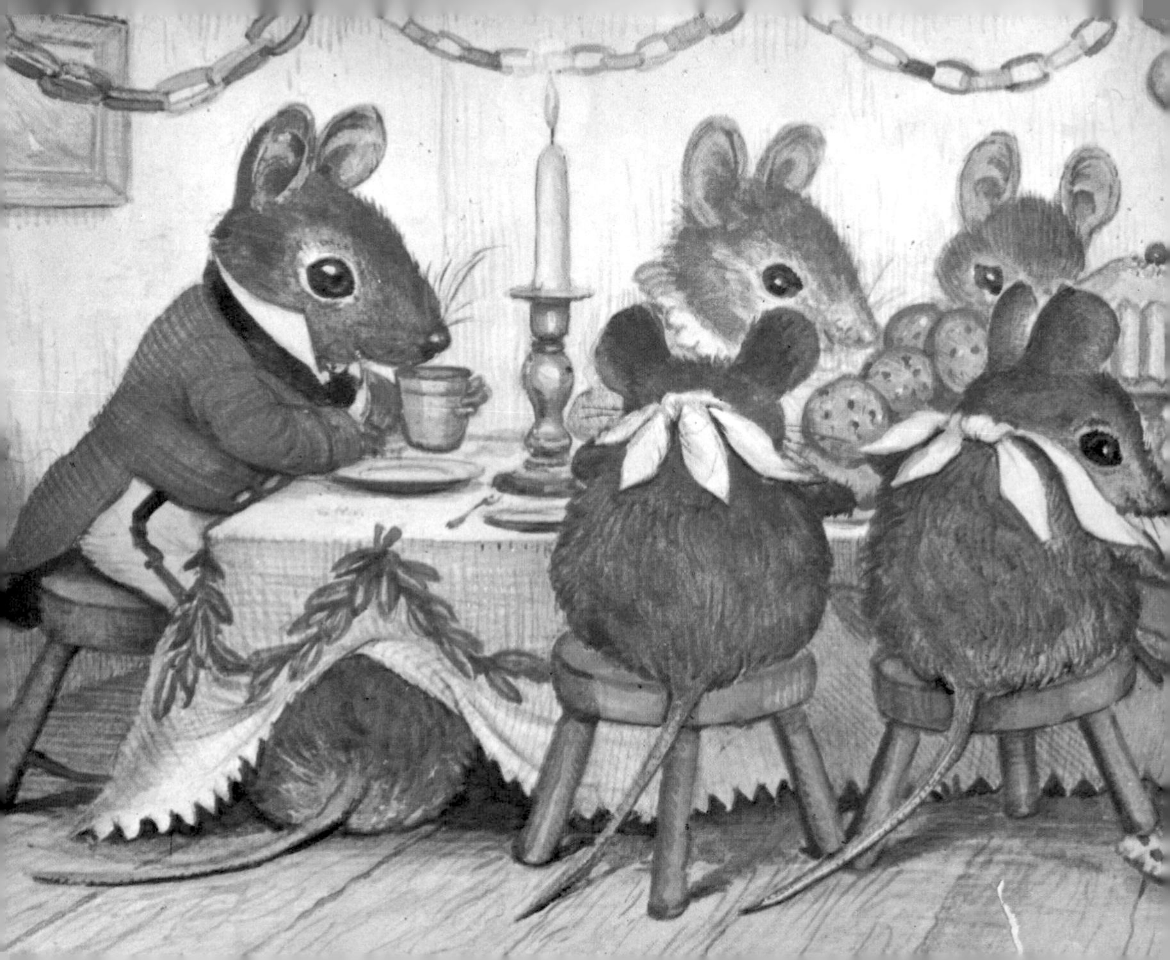

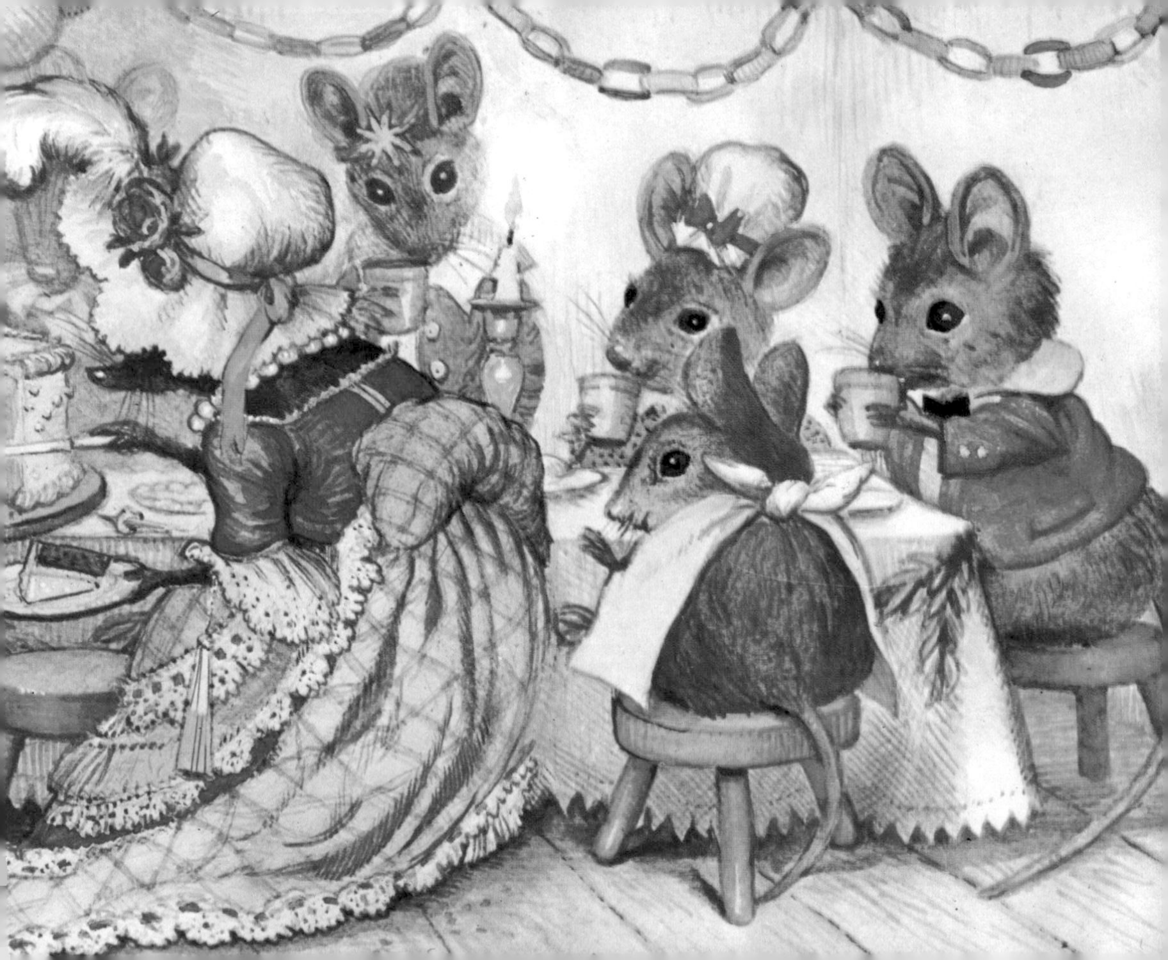

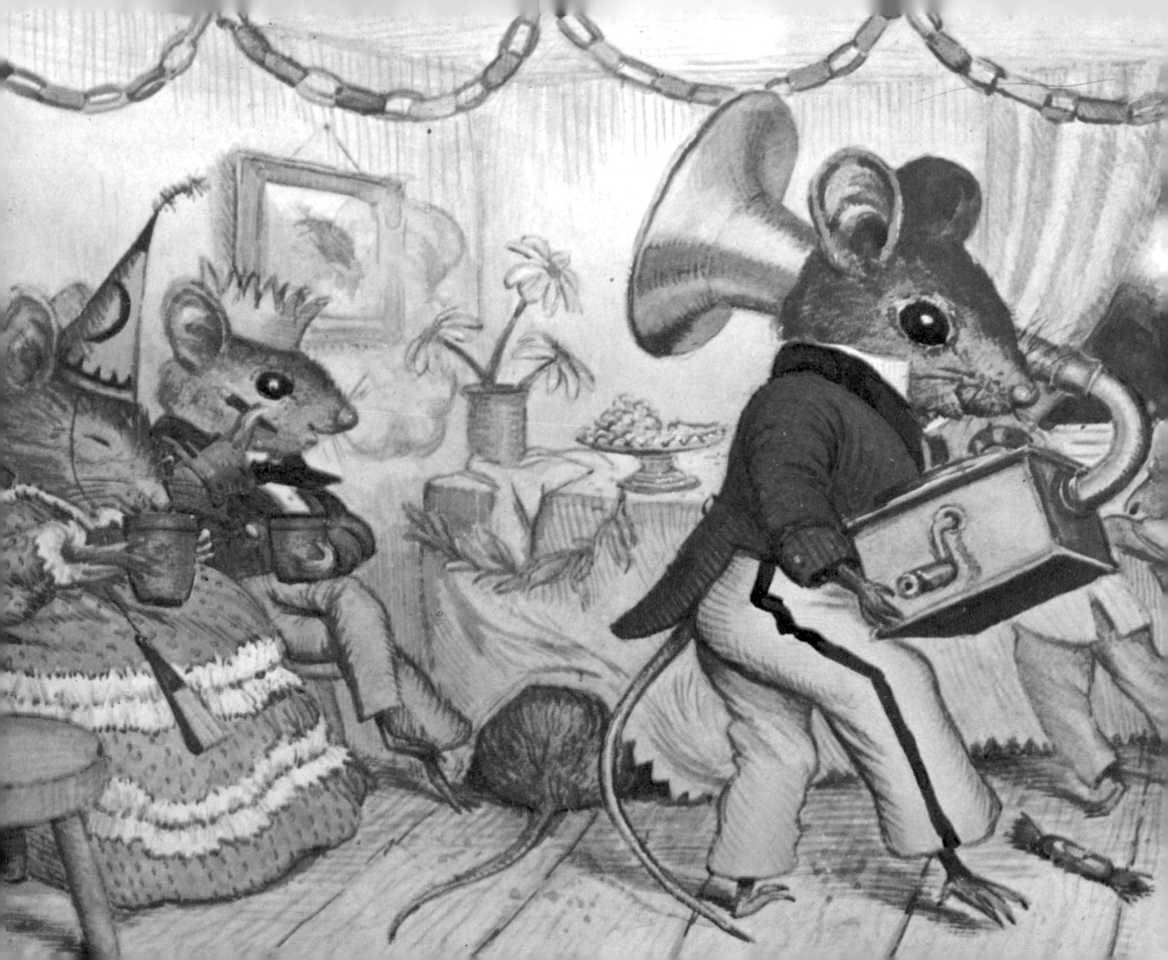

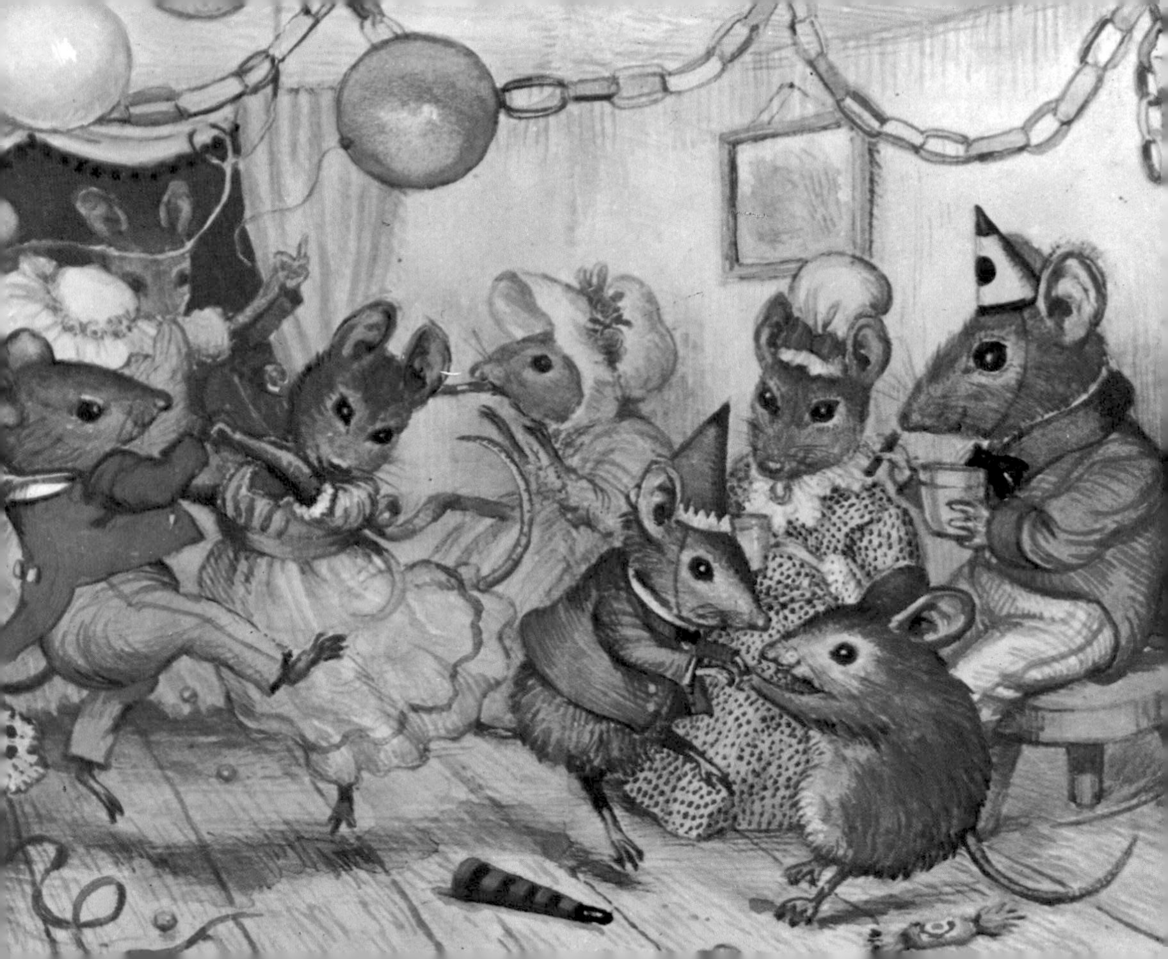

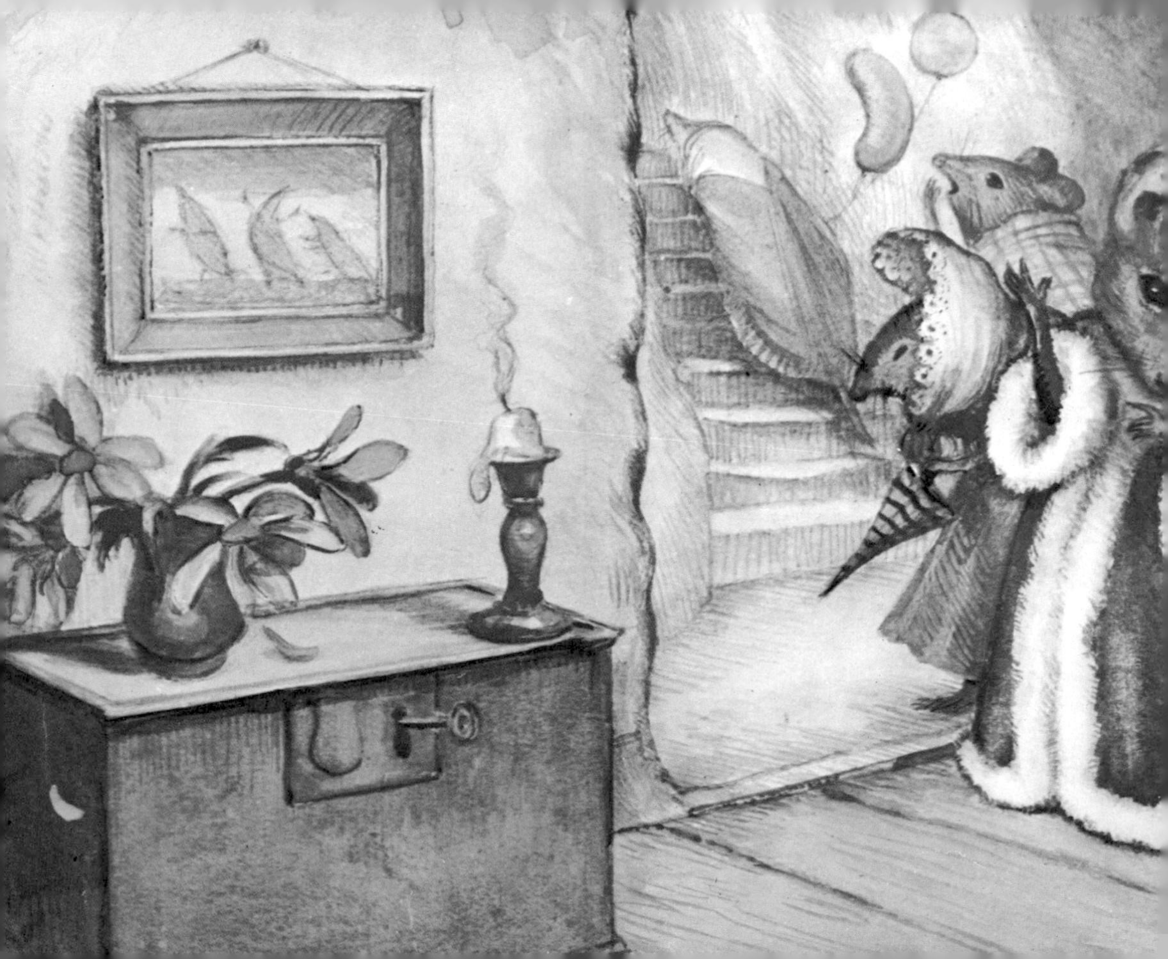

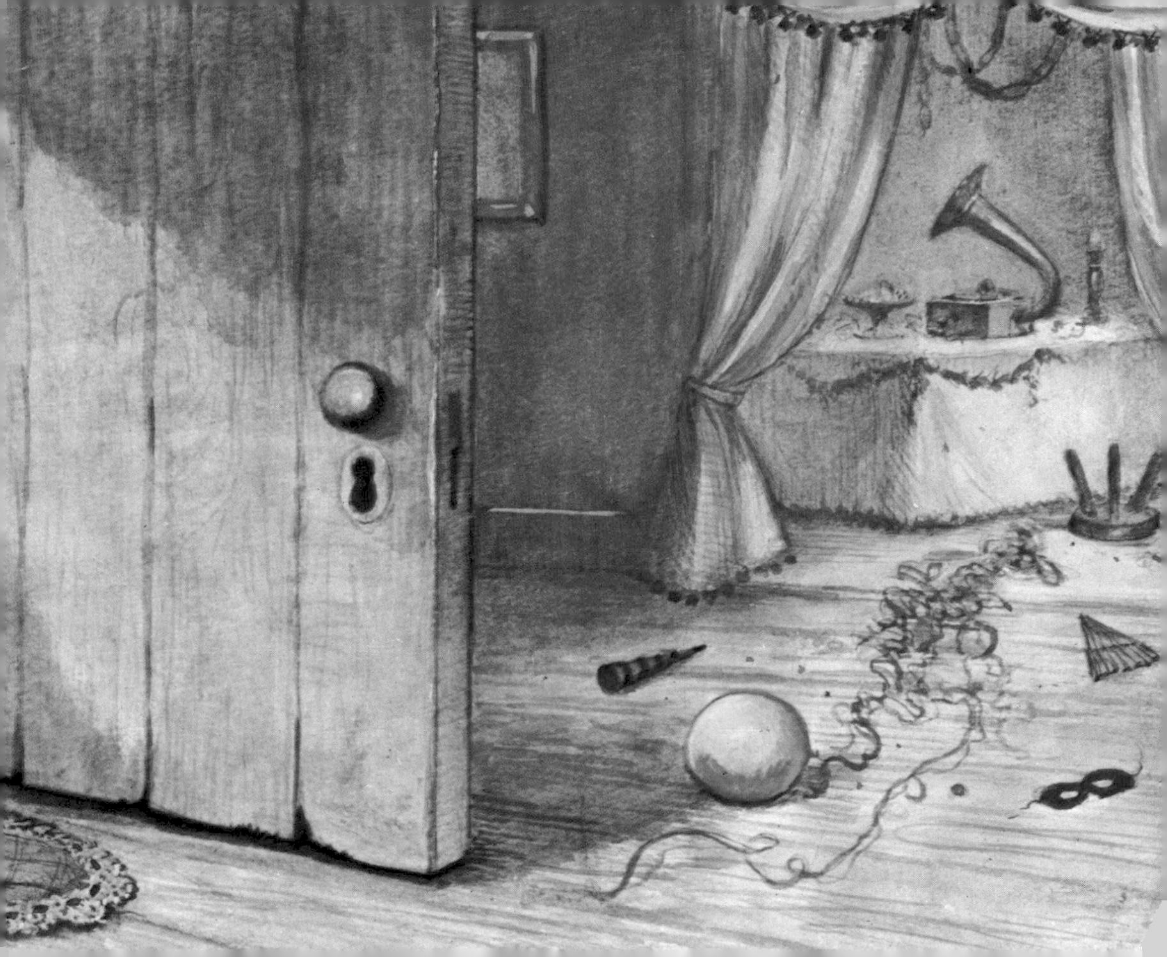

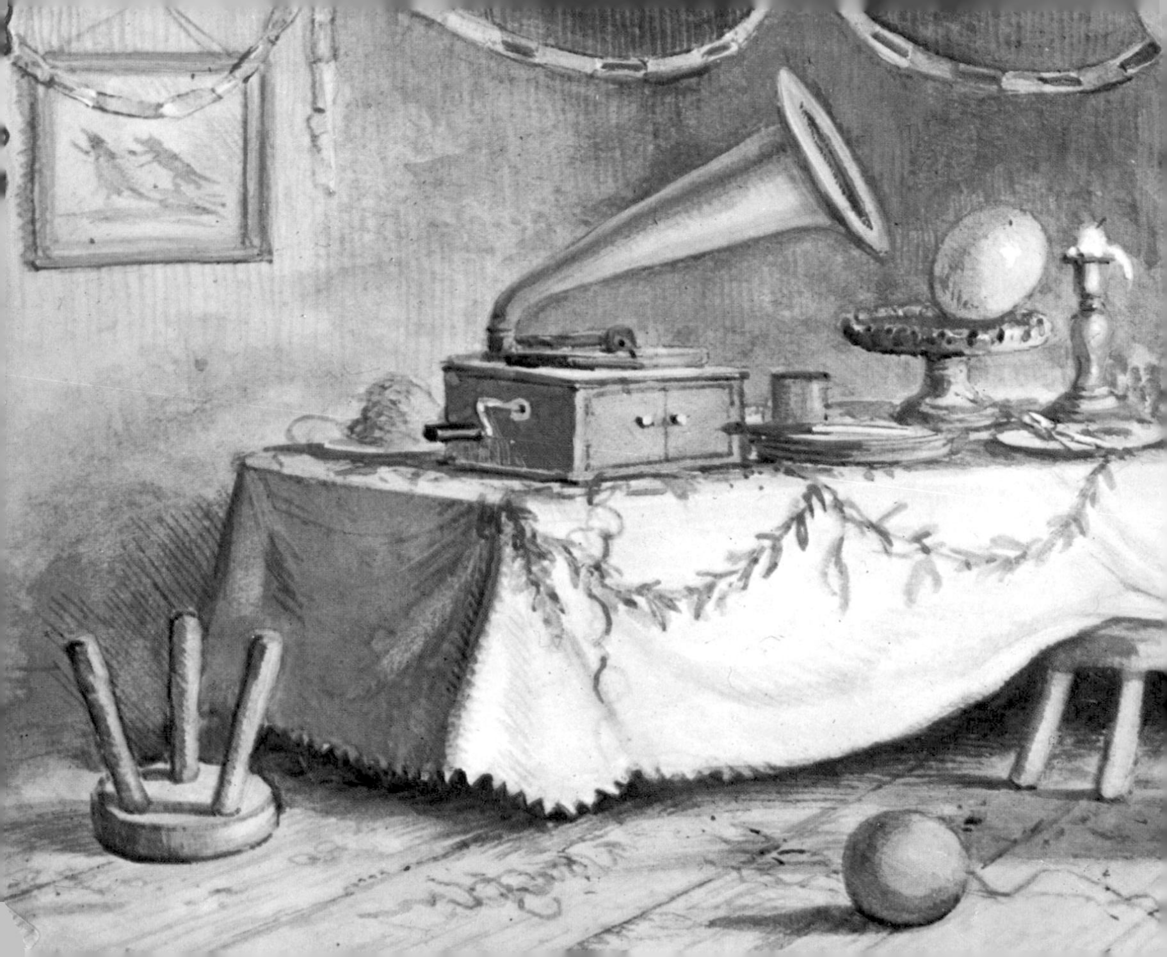

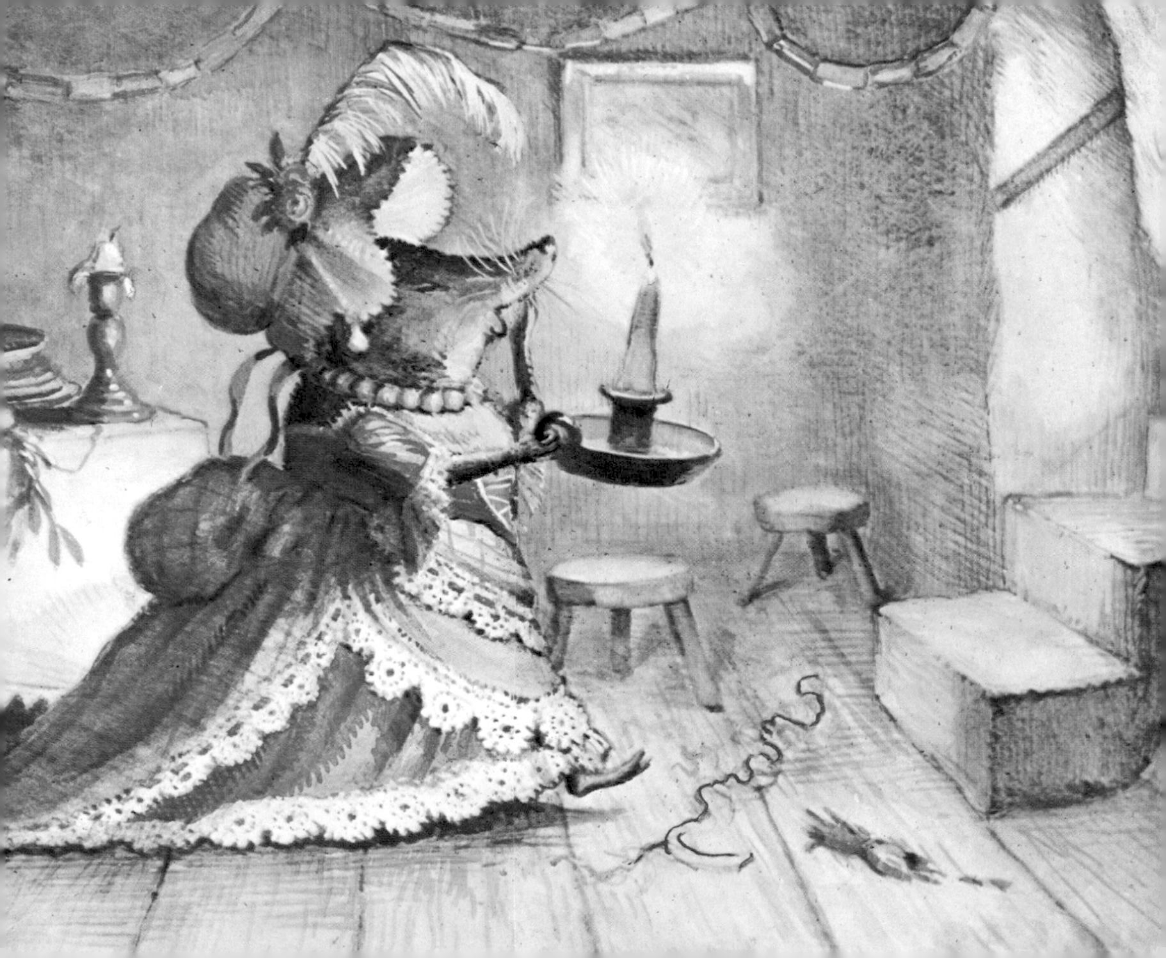

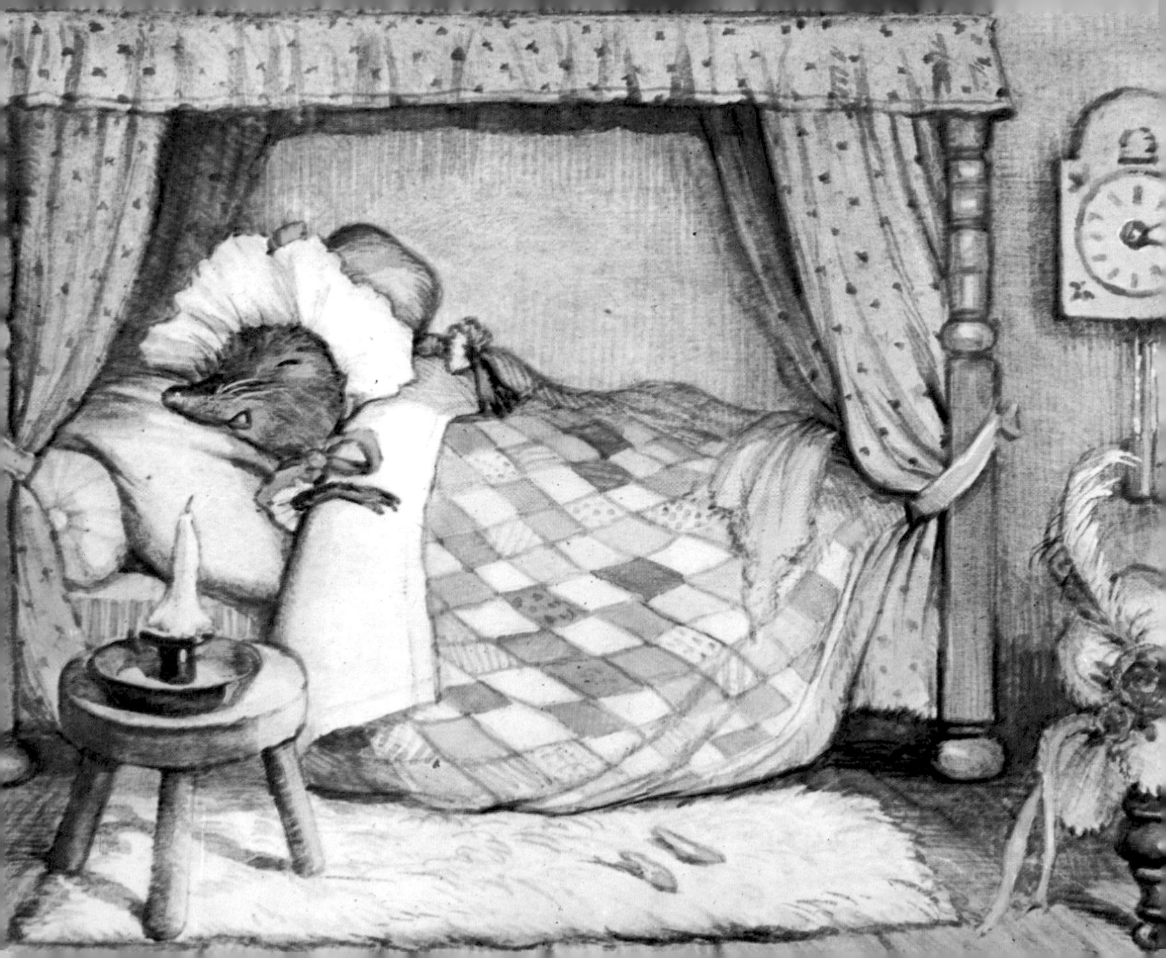